Crown Prince Marco suddenly felt very jaded.

Given a choice, he wouldn't marry anyone, much less notorious Princess Iliana.

But he didn't have a choice.

He'd come here to Dallas, Texas, to attend a charity ball and, at the same time, to meet the woman he had pledged to marry. He'd long ago promised King Mandrake that he would marry his daughter, and he meant to keep his word.

Marco was due to take over his rightful role as king very soon, and he would need a queen. Plus, his two motherless children needed a mother.

As a widower of two years, Marco had no appetite for the dating game. A ready-made mate would fit the bill for him.

As long as she didn't make too much trouble....

Dear Reader,

My, how time flies! I still remember the excitement of becoming Senior Editor for Silhouette Romance and the thrill of working with these wonderful authors and stories on a regular basis. My duties have recently changed, and I'm going to miss being privileged to read these stories before anyone else. But don't worry, I'll still be reading the published books! I don't think there's anything as reassuring, affirming and altogether delightful as curling up with a bunch of Silhouette Romance novels and dreaming the day away. So know that I'm joining you, even though Mavis Allen will have the pleasure of guiding the line now.

And for this last batch that I'm bringing to you, we've got some terrific stories! Raye Morgan is finishing up her CATCHING THE CROWN series with *Counterfeit Princess* (SR #1672), a fun tale that proves love can conquer all. And Teresa Southwick is just beginning her DESERT BRIDES trilogy about three sheiks who are challenged— and caught!—by American women. Don't miss the first story, *To Catch a Sheik* (SR #1674).

Longtime favorite authors are also back. Julianna Morris brings us *The Right Twin for Him* (SR #1676) and Doreen Roberts delivers *One Bride: Baby Included* (SR #1673). And we've got two authors new to the line—one of whom is new to writing! RITA® Award-winning author Angie Ray's newest book, *You're Marrying Her?*, is a fast-paced funny story about a woman who doesn't like her best friend's fiancée. And Patricia Mae White's first novel is about a guy who wants a little help in appealing to the right woman. Here *Practice Makes Mr. Perfect* (SR #1677).

All the best,

Mary-Theresa Hussey

Mary-Theresa Hussey
Senior Editor

Please address questions and book requests to:
Silhouette Reader Service
U.S.: 3010 Walden Ave., P.O. Box 1325, Buffalo, NY 14269
Canadian: P.O. Box 609, Fort Erie, Ont. L2A 5X3

COUNTERFEIT
PRINCESS
RAYE MORGAN

CATCHING
THE
CROWN

SILHOUETTE *Romance*®

Published by Silhouette Books

America's Publisher of Contemporary Romance

To Dallas—a great friend (and a wonderful city!)

SILHOUETTE BOOKS

RECYCLED PAPER

ISBN 0-373-19672-5

COUNTERFEIT PRINCESS

Copyright © 2003 by Helen Conrad

Visit Silhouette at www.eHarlequin.com

Printed in U.S.A.

RAYE MORGAN

has spent almost two decades, while writing over fifty novels, searching for the answer to that elusive question: Just what is that special magic that happens when a man and a woman fall in love? Every time she thinks she has the answer, a new wrinkle pops up, necessitating another book! Meanwhile, after living in Holland, Guam, Japan and Washington, D.C., she currently makes her home in Southern California with her husband and two of her four boys.

THE NABOTAVIAN ROYAL FAMILY

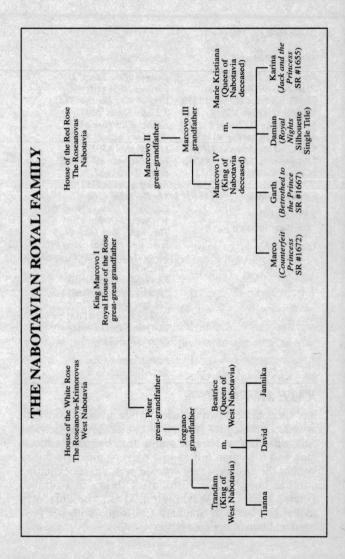

House of the White Rose
The Roseanova-Krimorovas
West Nabotavia

House of the Red Rose
The Roseanovas
Nabotavia

King Marcovo I
Royal House of the Rose
great-great grandfather

Peter
great-grandfather

Marcovo II
great-grandfather

Jorgano
grandfather

Marcovo III
grandfather

Trandam
(King of
West Nabotavia)

Beatrice
(Queen of West Nabotavia)

m.

Marcovo IV
(King of
Nabotavia
deceased)

Marie Kristiana
(Queen of Nabotavia
deceased)

m.

Tianna

David

Jannika

Marco
(*Counterfeit
Princess*
SR #1672)

Garth
(*Betrothed to
the Prince*
SR #1667)

Damian
(*Royal
Nights*
Silhouette
Single Title)

Karina
(*Jack and the
Princess*
SR #1655)

Chapter One

"All right, no more hedging, Jordan. Tell me what you've heard about Princess Iliana. And be specific. I want to know exactly what I'm getting into."

Nabotavia's Crown Prince Marco Roseanova was talking tough, giving his valet a measured look. He would trust the man with his life, but could he trust him to repeat the local gossip?

"I'm afraid she does seem to have a bit of a reputation, Your Highness."

Jordan looked pained as he said the words and Marco sighed, sure he was holding something back. "I need the facts if I'm going to do anything about this."

"They say she has a—" Jordan's long face was always mournful, but now it twisted as though he thoroughly disapproved of the scent of the aftershave lotion Marco was applying to his sleek and handsome face "—a gangster for a boyfriend."

Marco suddenly felt very tired. Given a choice, he wouldn't marry anyone, much less Princess Iliana with her notoriety. And he'd certainly been warned about her before from people very close to him. But he didn't have a choice. He'd come to Dallas, Texas to attend an annual charity ball the local Nabotavian community put on and at the same time, to meet the woman he had pledged to marry. He'd promised King Mandrake of Alovitia that he would marry his daughter and he meant to keep his word.

Marco was due to take over his rightful role as King of Nabotavia very soon, and by law he needed a queen. And his two motherless children needed a mother. As a widower of only two years he had no appetite for getting into the dating game. A ready-made mate would fit the bill for him right now. As long as she didn't make too much trouble.

"I think we'll be able to convince her to give up her less-savory hobbies," he said, reaching for his tuxedo jacket. "Let's go meet this wild child of a princess, shall we?"

Jordan dipped his head in acquiescence and turned to open the door for his employer. They rode the elevator down to the ballroom in silence, and as the doors slid open to reveal the crowd gathering on the landing, they exchanged a look and started for the entrance.

"It's the crown prince," someone said as they passed, and the crowd began to part, letting them through to the top of the stairs where the announcer was introducing each new set of arrivals over a speaker system.

"There she is," Jordan muttered to him suddenly. "Blue gown and tiara."

Marco looked across the landing and met a gaze so startlingly open in its curiosity, he was caught for a moment, unable to look away. She was beautiful, just as he remembered from ten years before. *That* he had expected. But he hadn't anticipated the clear gaze, the lifted chin, the lack of guile, the complete absence of either contrition or defiance. She could have been an angel. But he knew damn well she wasn't.

He blinked and finally he pulled his gaze away, reaching to tug on the constriction of the neck of his shirt. "I can't meet her yet," he told Jordan, turning back from the announcer and looking toward the bar. "I'm going to need a good stiff drink before I can handle this one."

He didn't bother to look at Jordan's face. He knew he would see disapproval. But a man could only do what he could do, and right now, too much was flooding in on him—memories, emotions. The princess was certainly lovely, but the face of his beloved Lorraine, the wife he'd lost too soon, was haunting him. That was enough to put a cold, painful grip on his heart. He needed a few minutes to himself. Squaring his shoulders, he strolled into the bar and nodded to the bartender.

"Well, Greta," said Shannon Harper, the woman Prince Marco had taken for the princess, speaking to one of the two Alovitian courtiers standing on either side of her as she watched Marco turn and head for the bar. "I'd say the prince has no more interest in meeting Princess Iliana than the real princess has in meeting him. Wouldn't you agree?''

''He's just a little nervous,'' the gray-haired countess murmured. ''He'll be back.'' But she was wringing her bejeweled hands and a half second later her true feelings came flooding out. She looked across Shannon to the short, bald man standing on the other side of her. ''Did you see the way he looked at her? Do you think he knew? He knew, didn't he? He could tell right away that she is an imposter!''

''Get a grip, Greta,'' Freddy muttered at her, carefully maintaining his dignified presence. ''And don't say that in public. You never know who is listening.'' He leaned closer to his cohort. ''He didn't notice a thing. He just wants a drink, that's all. You'll see. He'll be back.''

Shannon looked from one to the other of her handlers. She was getting darn tired of being treated like a mannequin whose only function was to smile and wave and pretend to be Princess Iliana of Alovitia. But that was exactly what she was being well-paid for.

Her strange adventure had started almost two months before when she'd been offered a mysterious job. She already had part-time work as a hostess at a steak house to pay for her graduate studies in art history. Greta and Freddy had found her there one night when they had come in for a meal. They introduced themselves as close advisors to the king of the obscure little country of Alovitia, sent to America to act as support for Princess Iliana. Exclaiming over Shannon's incredible resemblance to the king's daughter, they stunned her by saying they would pay her to pretend to be the princess.

"We will train you," Greta had told her when she resisted. "Princess Iliana is busy in another part of the country and not available for the many charitable functions she had promised to attend. You will take her place. No one will ever know the difference."

It was an interesting offer, especially because she had friend, family and professional ties to that area of Eastern Europe. She'd been reluctant at first, despite the fact that she had accrued large debts during her mother's long illness and knew the money being offered would come in very handy. "Won't anyone she knows realize I'm not her?"

"That's the beauty of it. She has only recently bought a ranch outside of town. The local Alovitian community has never really known her at all."

So she'd played the part that had taken her far from her ordinary life and catapulted her into a status that caused heads to turn. That had been intoxicating for a while, though there had been a lot of hard work involved, a lot of luncheons to attend, conferences to appear at, parades to grace with her presence, riding in an open car. After a few weeks, she'd begun to understand why the real princess had skipped out on her obligations. Which brought up another matter. She'd been hired on a short term, temporary basis. Wasn't it time for the princess to come home?

That question had come to the fore when Greta had told her about the ball, and the fact that Crown Prince Marco of Nabotavia was planning to attend as a way of reintroduction to the princess.

"I thought I would die when I heard he was going

to be coming to this ball to see her," Greta moaned dramatically at the time. "It's too soon. He's not supposed to come for another month. But I suppose he couldn't wait."

"Have you tried to get in touch with her?" Shannon had asked, wishing she could think of a graceful way to bail out of this assignment.

"Oh yes. We've combed Nevada from one end to the other. She's not to be found."

By now Shannon had come to understand that the absent princess was not in another part of the country ministering to the needs of orphans or anything remotely of the kind. She was rumored to be in Las Vegas living in the fast lane and defying her father at every turn.

"Well, I hope you know that this is the very last time I'm doing this," Shannon had said uneasily. "It's one thing to go cutting ribbons at supermarket openings and waving to the crowd. It's another to fool a man about the woman that he loves. Or that he's going to love. Or marry, anyway."

Even at the time she had been very much afraid that her luck in passing as faux royalty was about to be seriously tested. Now she knew she should have followed her instincts and quit the princess impersonation business while she had her chance.

"Here you go," Greta said, squeezing her hand as they found themselves at the front of the line, ready to be announced. "Good luck!" And she faded back into the crowd, leaving Shannon on Freddy's arm.

Shannon looked out at the waves of glittering patrons in the ballroom below and felt a surge of nerves. She'd never attended anything like this before. Put on by the Nabotavian Ladies Relief Society of Dallas, it was one of the most important events of the fall social calendar and everyone from local politicians to media celebrities were in attendance.

"Her Royal Highness, Princess Iliana and Count Frederich of Alovitia," the herald announced loudly. Faces turned all over the ballroom and a murmur ran through the crowd.

"Steady as she goes, my dear," Freddy whispered, patting her hand as it clutched the crook of his arm, bracing her as they descended the wide staircase. "You're going to do just fine."

Even for Dallas, the event was spectacular. The glitter of light from the chandeliers reflecting on the masses of precious gems adorning the women in attendance was blinding. Men and women alike were dressed to the nines, silk and satin predominating. The ballroom itself was stunning, its huge windows towering twenty feet high and draped with red velvet curtains held back with braided golden cords. A full orchestra was playing and people were dancing.

Freddy escorted her slowly around the floor and suddenly she realized that everywhere they turned, handsome young men were gaping in her direction. It gave her a start to see this sort of male reaction. She really wasn't used to it. Freddy and Greta had obviously done a good job in directing the hairdresser, the makeup artist and the costumer who'd worked on her for hours this afternoon. She'd thought she looked pretty good when she'd surveyed the results in her mirror. But the male gazes she was meeting here were a better confirmation.

Whatever the magicians who'd worked on her had

done had turned her limp, dishwater hair into a cascading tower of shiny blond locks piled gracefully atop her head, leaving lovely curling tendrils to float flatteringly around her face. The entire creation had been topped off with a tiara of drop pearls which now framed her forehead. The effect was…well, royal.

And amplified when they had poured her into a formfitting electric blue strapless gown and propped her into stilt-like shoes, draped her neck and earlobes with more exotic pearls, and turned her funny, freckled face into something out of a fashion magazine. How they'd done it, she didn't know. But it was definitely one of the better perks of pretending to be royal.

Crown Prince Marco's name was announced and Freddy turned her so that she could see him descending the stairs. Her pulse began to thump a little harder. This time she was probably going to have to meet him face-to-face.

She smiled and nodded to a passing matron who had addressed her, then looked back at Crown Prince Marco again. Dressed in a beautifully tailored tuxedo that fit his lean, wiry-looking body perfectly, he had none of the ornamentation of some of the men she'd noticed. But he didn't need that sort of thing to appear impressive. There was something in the set of his shoulders, the tilt of his head, the steady gaze from his brilliant blue eyes, that did that all on their own.

He was listening to a tall, raven-haired woman, who was obviously attempting a charm offensive, but though he looked polite, his gaze was wandering, and for just a moment, it met Shannon's across the heads of about twenty people between them. She looked away quickly and swallowed hard. This was not going to be as easy as it had seemed when they'd been planning the evening. How was she going to get away with pretending to be the woman this man was going to marry?

"Just wait here," Freddy told her quietly, observing the scene. "Let him come to you."

So she waited, heart beating a bit faster than usual. And in a moment, he appeared, standing before her, looking like the prince he was. Up close, he was even more impressive. Handsome in a rugged way, his face had a rather gaunt look, as though he'd witnessed many unpleasant acts in his past that he would like to forget, but couldn't.

She knew he was a widower. Was that what accounted for the haunted look in his eyes? She didn't know, but his dignified reserve only made him more challenging. Her mouth went dry as he nodded to Freddy, then turned his full attention to her.

"Princess," he said, giving her a deep bow, his gaze cool though his lips were tilted in a slight smile.

"Your Royal Highness." She curtsied and held out her hand to him. He took it and brushed her fingers lightly with his lips.

She'd had her hand kissed before. Freddy had been putting her through the paces, practicing how to do it with a casualness that would bespeak royal breeding. At the appearances she'd been attending, men had been snacking on her fingers for weeks. But this was different.

His lips touched her skin and a shock of response shot through her, more like heat than electricity.

"Oh!" she said involuntarily, trying to jerk her hand back.

But he held on to it and looking up, he caught her stunned expression before she could hide it. A look of bemused surprise lit his silver blue eyes.

"Why Princess Iliana, you are looking more beautiful even than I remembered you," he told her as he finally released her hand.

She knew what came next. After all, she'd practiced it. She was supposed to say, "And you as well, Your Royal Highness," or something neat and polite such as that. Instead, she heard herself stammer, "I am?" feeling a fool.

His mouth twisted but she couldn't tell if that was supposed to be a smile or not. If so, it certainly hadn't reached his eyes.

"I suppose we must dance," he said, looking at the dance floor with something less than enthusiasm.

"Must we?" she said, alarmed.

Just a few words, they'd told her. You'll barely be introduced, then we'll whisk you away. What on earth was this talk of dancing?

"I don't know if you remember how much I hate it," he added.

She gazed up into his face with naked relief. "Oh…if you'd rather not…"

He gave her a quizzical look, one eyebrow raised. "You mean you would let me off the hook?" he said, as though he could hardly believe she could say such a thing.

"Of course." And gladly. She looked around for Freddy. If only she could escape!

But the prince stepped closer and looked down at

her. "For some reason, Princess," he said softly, "I find you a little too anxious to get rid of me." His eyes glittered with something she hoped was humor, but she couldn't tell for sure. He held out his elbow. "Shall we?"

Help did not seem to be on the way and she gave in to the inevitable. Remembering to keep her head high, she gave him the slightest of nods and slipped her hand into the crook of his arm as they made their way toward the dance floor.

With a small mental shrug, she turned to face him. She'd signed on for smiling and waving, and a few sentences into a microphone here and there. She'd never bargained on dancing with a prince. But his arms came around her and the music seemed to swell, and they were off.

"Just let me get through this," she thought to herself, feeling awkward and phony and out of her depth, "and I'll go to the powder room and stay until Freddy says we can go home."

But even as she thought the words, she caught sight of herself in one of the long mirrored panels between the high windows, and for just a second, she wondered who that beautiful princess was. It was seeing the crown prince in the mirror as well that brought the truth home to her. They looked like they belonged in a fairy tale. Both of them.

Her head went just a little higher. What the heck. If through some miracle she had managed to look like a princess, surely she could make a little more effort to act like one. Forget Shannon Harper. Shannon was gone. History. Someone new was taking her place. For now.

"My name is Princess Iliana," she thought to herself. "I am royal, darn it! And I'm not going to forget it."

Consciously, she made herself relax in the prince's arms. She jutted her chin out just a bit more, let the rhythm of the music loosen her knees just a bit more, and then she did the most important thing. She made herself to look up into his face and smile.

He didn't smile back, but his grip on her tightened and his hand slid higher and spread across the naked area below her shoulder blades, radiating heat across her skin.

He wasn't saying anything. At first she was relieved, but after a moment or two of silence, it finally registered that he was being incredibly patronizing. After all, he was supposed to be wooing her, wasn't he? Not just putting in time on a schedule. The nerve of the man—she was a princess!

Looking up into his eyes again, she gave him a more knowing smile. Now that her confidence had been revived, she managed to shed most of her awkwardness.

"After the way you turned from me on the landing, I was afraid I wasn't going to actually meet with you," she said, her tone playfully accusatory. "So kind of you to spare me a moment or two."

His mouth barely quirked at the corners. "I took one look at you and felt the need of a little liquid courage, I'm afraid," he admitted, though his tone belied his words.

"You're kidding," she said, truly incredulous. "Is it women in general that bother you? Or just this particular princess?"

"It isn't the woman. It's the situation." His glance in her direction said that he wasn't used to this sort of challenge and wasn't sure what to make of it. "Doesn't this situation bother you?"

"Not a bit," she said with all honesty. After all, she wasn't the one who was going to have to marry him. And if anyone thought she would sign on for that duty, they could think again. Marriage had never been her goal.

"Then, 'You're a better man than I am, Gunga Din,'" he muttered, mostly to himself.

She frowned. She was getting the distinct impression that he thought a conversation with his own alter ego would be more stimulating than any chat he might have with her. Prince or no prince, she wasn't going to let him get away with that.

"If you're going to start spouting Rudyard Kipling, you'd better watch out. I just might give you some Emily Dickinson in return."

His eyes widened as he looked down at her. "What? A princess with an education in literature? This is something new."

A flush of pleasure surged through her as she saw an actual spark of interest ignite in his gaze. "Ah," she said wisely. "So the real problem is finally revealed. You have no respect for princesses."

"Not true. My very favorite sister is a princess."

"Family never counts, though, does it?" she noted, wrinkling her nose.

"On the contrary, family is the only thing that counts."

She opened her mouth, then closed it again. This was certainly a different way of looking at things than she was used to. But she supposed royalty had to think that way. Family was, after all, their claim to fame. "I guess you're very proud of yours, aren't you?"

"Of course. Aren't you proud of yours?"

She made a face. "Not in the way you're talking about. After all, family is just something you're handed at birth. What you do with it is what counts. The sort of person you become."

He held her slightly away so that he could take a good look at her face. "I've heard a lot about the woman you've become, Princess, but no one had warned me you were a philosopher."

She wanted to ask just what he had heard, but then she remembered they weren't really talking about her. Before she could think of anything else to say, the music faded. The dance was over and she sighed with relief, turning her head to look for Freddy. It took a moment to register the fact that the prince hadn't let go of her, and when the music began again, and his arms seemed to tighten around her, she realized her ordeal had not yet come to its logical conclusion.

But another thought pushed that disappointment aside. She hadn't let it fully sink in yet, but she was dancing with the crown prince of Nabotavia! Despite the circumstances, this was a dream come true. Her concentration in her art history studies was in Eastern European Art of the Twentieth Century, with an emphasis on Nabotavia. For the last two years she'd read everything she could get her hands on about the plucky little country, studying its history, immersing herself in its art work. She'd tried to keep current on the fight to oust the radicals, though there hadn't been much in the local press. And now here she was with the prince.

Her heart gave a little leap, but she stilled it. She had to remain calm. After all, a princess of the next-door country wouldn't think this was any big deal, now would she?

Stay calm. Stay natural. Think of something to say.

"Have you changed your opinion of dancing?" she asked as they swayed to a rhythmic arrangement of a classical tune.

"No," he told her. "But I am in the process of revising my opinion of you."

Something in his tone, something in the way he was looking down at her, sent a riff of sensation cascading down her spine and she almost gasped aloud.

Wow. Where had that come from?

But she already knew the answer. The music was creating a sumptuous background to the night, along with the shimmering lights and the richly dressed crowd. That helped. The scent of candles and gardenias filled the air, creating a scene for magic, a backdrop for fairy tales. A girl could lose her head in a setting like this.

But even more important was the spectacularly handsome man who held her. At first she'd been impressed with his looks and his royal bearing. But now something else was throwing her off her stride. Suddenly she was conscious of the flesh-and-blood man beneath the regalia, and that sense of awareness flooded her with a feeling a little too intense for the circumstances.

Blinking, she swallowed hard and stared at his tux lapel. This prince was also a man, a very muscular man, with wide shoulders and a masculine scent that was suddenly filling her head. His hand on her skin seemed to sizzle. His warm breath tickled her ear. His hard thigh grazed the inside of her leg as they made a turn and an aching longing seemed to curl like smoke up through her body.

She bit down hard on the inside of her lip. If she didn't stop this impossible swoon, she was going to melt into a puddle of ridiculous eroticism right here on the dance floor. Taking a deep breath, she forced herself back into sanity, hardening her resistance, coming up for air.

You will not fall for this man, she told herself fiercely. Now stick with the program and fend off all feelings of fatal attraction.

There. She sighed with relief. She'd done it. And though it seemed like forever since she'd swooned, he was looking at her as though he were still waiting for an answer to his statement, so it couldn't have lasted as long as she'd thought.

Now, what had he said? Oh yes.

I am in the process of revising my opinion of you.

It was certainly a statement that needed a response of some kind.

Chapter Two

"So you arrived tonight with a skeptical opinion of me?" Shannon asked, her firm tone masking her wobbly confidence. "And just where did you form it? We haven't seen each other for ten years." Or so she'd been told in the short lecture on facts Greta had given her just hours before.

"Over ten years," Marco agreed. "The last time I saw you I believe was the night we danced at your debutante ball when you were sixteen."

"Really?" Oh-oh. Now she'd done it. This was her worst fear, that he would bring up the past, a past she knew absolutely nothing about.

"You don't remember?"

She shook her head quickly. "I'm sorry. I'm afraid I've got amnesia for anything that happened before I turned twenty-one." Hah! A master stroke, if she did say so herself.

"Oh really?" His dark eyebrow rose in surprise.

He made no effort to pretend to believe her. "Damned convenient, isn't it?"

She gave him a superior look. That was her story and she was sticking to it. But she felt a prickly sense of irritation that he seemed so ready to think the worst of her. She wanted to react to his dry tone with a sharp retort, but she stopped herself in time. She had to remember what was going on here. This was not a real relationship with a real man. This was playacting.

And she wasn't supposed to be involved in it, darn it all! She had to watch what she said and hope to get out of this without being unmasked. Looking into his eyes, she searched for evidence that he had suspicions about her. But all she saw were shadows hiding any emotion he might be feeling. If he did feel anything at all. Which she was beginning to doubt.

The trouble was, she *did* feel things. Sometimes she seemed to be a fountain of feeling, spilling out all over the place. Instinct told her she was already beginning to feel a very inappropriate list of things about this man. And wouldn't that just land her in a pickle if she didn't watch it? Not only was he a prince, while she was a phony, paid by the hour, but his hard jaw and ice-cold gaze told her he wouldn't melt for a mere woman. Not on a bet.

"Amnesia runs in my family," she told him airily, deciding nonsense was better than trying to stick to facts. "We all get it sooner or later."

He nodded, looking slightly bored. "I understand," he said. "The truth is often difficult to face."

Her eyes narrowed as she looked up at him. Was

he baiting her? "And you think you know the truth about me?" she asked slowly.

His smile didn't reach his eyes. "I seem to know more of it than you do. You have amnesia. Remember?"

She bit her lip. Score one for the arrogant prince. Now she was really annoyed, but that was certainly less dangerous than swooning.

"What I remember most about our last meeting was, actually, the dancing," he went on. "You dance much better now than you did then. As I recall, your spike heels gouged holes in my feet that didn't heal for weeks."

"I'm so sorry," she told him unconvincingly. And then she couldn't resist a quick follow-up. "But I think you'd have to admit, at least a part of the credit goes to now having a partner who has finally learned how to lead."

He gazed at her questioningly. "I thought you didn't remember anything from the past."

She waved a hand in the air. "I don't. I'm just extrapolating from current evidence."

"Oh, I see." His face finally registered the fact that she was purposely trying to get his goat. "So you find my dancing just barely adequate at this point?"

She smiled, glad to know he was feeling her jabs at last but still not sure if he was taking them with humor or annoyance. "I didn't say that at all."

His blue eyes glittered. "No, but you certainly implied it."

"Assumptions are risky things."

"I guess I lead a dangerous life, then." His eyebrow quirked. "Speaking of which…"

She could tell by his tone that he was leading into something she wasn't going to like and she steeled herself.

"I hear you've been leading quite an interesting life since I saw you last. Perhaps you might find time at some future date to fill me in on the particulars of anything I might need to know."

She saw right through him. What was he angling for, an abject apology from the princess that she'd been around the block a few times? Despite the gossip she'd heard about Iliana, and the things she knew about her as well, she felt an impulse to defend her. But she held it back. After all, she wasn't here to build foundations for their future relationship. She was just here to smile and get through the evening without creating a disaster.

"A gentleman doesn't ask a lady things about her past," she said evasively, her glance into his eyes just short of a glare.

His dark eyebrow rose again. "In my experience, that rule only applies when the past is somewhat shady."

"Shady!"

"Well, cloudy at the very least."

"Really?" Anger could easily turn to fury if she didn't watch it. She choked back her impulse to go on the attack for a moment, but then couldn't resist one quick comment. "I suppose your past is pure as the driven snow."

"My past is irrelevant," he said, looking infuriatingly superior. "But your reaction tells me all I need to know about yours."

"Oh really?" The man was insufferable! "A lot

you know. Give me one example of something 'cloudy' in the prin…in my past.'' She knew the moment the words were on her lips that she was courting disaster but she couldn't stand the way he was lording it over her.

''You wouldn't like me to do that.''

''You're bluffing,'' she challenged hotly, and dancing was forgotten as she stood glaring at him, chin out, hands on her hips. ''You don't have one.''

He gave her a long-suffering look. ''Your Highness, I hardly think this is the time or the place for this sort of display.''

''There.'' She tossed her head. ''I knew you didn't really have one.''

His cold gaze settled on her in a way that made her want to take a step backward, but she forced herself to hold her position.

''All right,'' he said slowly. ''I'll tell you of one. Although, as you have reminded me, it is very impolite for a gentleman to do so.''

''Have at it.''

Taking her arm and forcing a smile in the direction of a person he recognized, he led her quickly away from the crowd and out onto a balcony where they could have at least the semblance of privacy. Once alone, she swung around to face him, and he began his reminiscence.

''The time I'm thinking of was when you must have been about fourteen. All our families were congregated at that resort in the south of France. I was in a sailing race when I found you, barely dressed in a thong bikini you must have stolen from some street-walker, stowed away in my Laser. Of course, you ruined my chances in the race, and when I put you ashore, you told everyone who would listen that I'd kidnapped you.''

She winced inside, but would have died rather than show it. Princess Iliana did seem to have a penchant for inappropriate behavior. Her own inclination would have been to apologize, but she had to think what the real princess would say to having her adolescent idiocies thrown in her face. So she faced him with defiance.

''Did I also tell them you had no sense of humor?'' She shrugged grandly, turning to look out over the city street below where traffic was strung out like diamonds on a chain. ''Anyway, you made that up. I wouldn't ever have done such a thing.'' And that was true on a personal level.

''It was you or someone who looks a lot like you,'' he said, and her eyes widened, wondering for a second or two if he was wise to her. But he went on, adding, ''I've thought of a lot more instances, now that you've brought them to mind. Would you like to hear another?''

She waved a hand in the air, dismissing his suggestion. ''Unnecessary. I think I've got the general trend of the way your mind works.''

''So you do concede my point.''

''I don't concede anything.''

''That's illogical. You've basically conceded.''

''No I haven't.'' She turned to go back into the ballroom. ''But I'm through talking about it.''

He put an arm out, hand against the wall, blocking her passage. ''Concede,'' he demanded, his arrogance on proud display.

She stared up at him, aware once again of his wide shoulders and strong jaw. This was exactly the sort of man she had dreamed of in her adolescence, the sort of man who might grab a girl and throw her over his shoulder.... She shivered. What a ridiculous thought. She was adolescent no longer and she didn't dream of macho men. They were passe, old hat, from another time. The ideal man should respect a woman and treat her just the way he would a casual friend. The prince was out of line as far as she was concerned.

She glared at him. "You can't make me. You're not a king yet, you know."

"No," he agreed, his eyes narrowing. "But I'm sure to become one. And whether or not you become a queen is still up in the air, isn't it?"

She gasped. Turning back toward the balcony railing, she began to stroll, forcing him to follow her. "I don't know why you want to marry me if you really can't stand me."

He looked stunned that she would come right out and say it. "I never said any such thing."

"Your body language says it loud and clear."

"Then you are misreading my body."

Their gazes clashed, held for a long moment as they both digested the words he'd just spoken. Shannon felt heat flood her face, infuriating her even further. She quickly looked away. But they didn't resume walking, and in a few seconds, their eyes met again, as though it was impossible for them to keep from doing it.

"I just want you to know," Marco added roughly,

"that I wouldn't marry any woman that I couldn't stand."

She nodded crisply. "So the wedding is off?" she said, coolly searching his gaze.

He stared down at her as though she'd said something too outlandish to deal with, and suddenly Freddy was there, obsequiously inserting himself into the conversation. Shannon didn't actually hear what he was saying. She was still staring into Marco's gaze, wondering how she could be so angry with someone she found so attractive. But a moment later, she was leaving the balcony on Freddy's arm, forcing herself to resist the urge to look back at the crown prince.

"I am not marrying that man," she said through gritted teeth once she was alone with Greta in the dressing room. She saw the look that passed over Greta's face and she added quickly, "And if Princess Iliana is smart, she won't either."

Funny, but she hadn't spent much time wondering about the real Iliana before. The woman had hardly seemed real to her anyway. This was just a job she was doing. But now she had to face the fact that she'd been saying things in Iliana's name, things that might last and have repercussions, and that fact made everything very different.

She was pacing the floor in pent-up frustration and Greta was watching her as though she were witnessing a natural phenomenon that threatened disaster but couldn't be controlled. She stopped in front of the woman.

"You know, I'm going to have to talk to the princess when she gets back, before she meets with the prince. I'm going to have to tell her some of the things I've said to him. That is, if you all care about a smooth transition.''

She frowned. She knew Greta and Freddy were adamant that the princess would marry Marco. Their king had decreed it should be so and they were supposed to be making sure all went well. The fact that Iliana wasn't cooperating was still a secret to most people. Greta had assured her that Iliana would come through when the chips were down—but weren't they pretty much on the table at this point? And where was she?

Shannon shook her head, appealing to the woman's common sense. ''I don't see how this is going to work. Once he sees her, isn't he going to know she isn't me?''

Greta shrugged helplessly, looking miserable. ''What can we do? He is leaving tomorrow and won't be back for a few weeks. By then, maybe the impression you've made will fade. We will hope that he will attribute differences to her not having the makeup and not being dressed for a ball.'' Her hand went to her throat, diamonds sparkling. ''But her voice…her demeanor.'' She rolled her eyes. ''Well, he is bound to think something is different. But we didn't have much choice, did we? We had to take the chance.''

Shannon hesitated as a thread of guilt began to slither through her. She knew that Greta and Freddy were both scared to death of their employer, the king of Alovitia. She wasn't sure if they were just afraid for their jobs and position in the royal scheme of things, or if they actually feared for their own physical safety. And she was afraid that her own performance tonight wasn't going to help things where they were concerned.

"You know, we had a dreadful fight," she told the poor woman. "I said some things I probably shouldn't have said." She gave her a look of regret. "He may want to call the marriage off, I don't know."

Greta's eyes widened and she grabbed Shannon's arm. "What did you do? The king will have my head for this!"

Shannon swallowed hard and blinked back some misery of her own. "I'm sorry. I shouldn't have…"

"You must go back and make up with him." Greta thrust her hand toward the door, bracelets jangling. "Now. Hurry!"

Shannon shook her head. "Oh no, Greta. I can't do that. If you'd seen the way he looked at me…."

"Looks? You think that looks can hurt you?" She slapped the flat of her hand down on the table, her eyes almost wild. "The king will have more than looks waiting for me, I can tell you that. Why do you think he sent us here? We were to make sure his daughter bent to his will. This wedding must come about. It is King Mandrake's command that it be so." She put her hands together as though in prayer. "Please. Shannon. You must go back and make it up. You don't understand how important this is."

Shannon sighed. "You don't understand how hard it would be," she said softly. But she glanced into the mirror and caught a wayward strand of hair, already preparing for what she knew she had to do.

* * *

Crown Prince Marco paced the thick carpets of his hotel room, fuming as he went back over the conversation with the princess in his mind. "I don't know if we can believe those rumors, Jordan. Even gangsters have standards."

"Sir?"

He stopped to look at his valet in exasperation. "She's exactly the sort of woman I never could stand. Has to make a smart remark about everything you say." He threw up a hand. "Of course, maybe a gangster is the only type who likes that sort of thing."

"Indeed, sir."

Turning away and then quickly turning back again, he looked his valet in the eye. "Tell me, really, where did you hear those things about her?"

Jordan shrugged. "One hears things, Your Royal Highness. The other servants talk."

He nodded. "Well, I can't say I hadn't heard the rumors before myself. Lady Judith has told me much the same sort of gossip."

Sinking into a chair at the small round table, he put his head in his hands and closed his eyes. He hated this. If only Lorraine were still alive....

But she wasn't, and he had to go on. Ruthlessly, he pushed the picture of her sweet face out of his mind. He didn't have the time or the luxury to dwell on what might have been. He had a country to lead. Nabotavia needed a queen and needed King Mandrake's help on their western border. Marrying Princess Iliana would give them both those things.

She certainly wasn't his ideal. He couldn't even conceive of living with her as husband and wife. But he didn't imagine they would actually spend much time together, and he didn't need any more children. The ones he had were being well brought up by their grandmother, Judith, Lorraine's mother. A good step-mother for his children would have been nice, but one couldn't have everything one wanted in life. Often, one barely got what one needed.

Did he really need this woman?

Not personally. He'd managed without female companionship for the last two years. He couldn't claim that he'd done fine. He'd missed Lorraine every moment, ached for her. But in every other way, life had continued without much hassle. The children loved their grandmother. They still had the same nanny they had known since birth. As the crown prince, and soon as king, he had never been destined to be much of a hands-on father to them. That was something he regretted, but it couldn't be helped. He'd spent a good part of the last year fighting to free Nabotavia, and he would spend the rest of his life fighting to maintain that freedom for his country. Whether or not he was married would make little difference there.

But his country needed a queen, and his alliance with Alovitia was supremely important. So yes, much as he hated to admit it, he needed this woman. Slowly, he raised his head and looked at Jordan, misery shining in his eyes.

"Why can't my life be simple?" he asked him with a growl.

"Because you were born to a complex role, sir," Jordan answered sensibly.

Marco nodded. "I'm afraid you're right." He grimaced and swore softly. "I know I can't betray Mandrake after all he did to help me. If it hadn't been for him, Nabotavia would not be free."

"Quite true, sir."

Marco frowned. He'd never given much thought to why King Mandrake might want so badly to have his daughter married to him. He'd always supposed it was to strengthen ties with Nabotavia. The bonds between the two countries were ancient and would always be there, but would be vastly strengthened by a marriage between the two ruling houses. But maybe there was more. After all, she was at least twenty-eight by now, though she looked younger. And still unmarried. Her father was probably having a hard time getting anyone suitable to take her.

"If I might make a suggestion, sir."

He looked up hopefully. "Suggestions are welcomed, Jordan."

"It is well said that King Mandrake does have a terrible temper."

"A terrible temper. Yes indeed." Marco laughed softly and ran his fingers through his hair. "You know, Jordan, I'm thinking of developing a terrible temper when I'm king. What do you think?"

"Such a thing can come in handy, sir. But about my thoughts on tonight's subject."

"Yes. Go ahead."

"I believe I mentioned the king's temper. If he hears that you threw aside his daughter after ten minutes on the dance floor, he is liable to take it as an affront."

"Yes, I'm afraid you're right on that one. I can't do it, much as I may be tempted." His sigh came from deep in his heart.

"If you were to spend a few hours with the young lady, it is just possible that you may come to understand her better and even like her."

Marco coughed skeptically. "I get your drift, Jordan. And I know you are quite right." His spirit revived a bit. After all, if Jordan thought there was hope, there just might be at least a glimmer. "So I'm afraid I'm going to have to give it another go."

"If you feel it quite necessary, sir."

He nodded solemnly. "I do, Jordan." Turning toward the door, he squared his shoulders. "It is only fair to give the young woman another chance. Then, who knows?"

"Precisely, sir."

The interesting thing was that Princess Iliana seemed to have much the same idea as Crown Prince Marco did and was waiting with her two attendants very near the dance floor. She had something of a reluctant look on her face, as though it had taken a lot of persuading to get her to come back and meet with him again, but he didn't care. As long as she was available, he would do what he could to repair the damage of their earlier meeting, and hopefully, build a common relationship. If it was possible to make it a friendly collaboration, that would be best. But if he had to throw her over his shoulder and carry her down the aisle, he'd do it. Bottom line, he was going to marry her.

He studied her as he came closer. She really was beautiful, with a rare luminous quality, as though she were lit with a warm light from within. For just a moment, he felt a slight pang of regret. If only she'd been a different sort of woman, he was sure something could have been worked out. But as she was, he could only hope for miracles.

He bowed and smiled and murmured a few pleasantries. She nodded and gave him a tight smile back, and as she came to join him on the dance floor, she glanced back at her attendants with a look he couldn't read. Rebellion? Desperation? Threats of revenge? He wasn't sure. But it didn't matter, just as long as she agreed to put in some time with him. For all he knew, she might be as determined as he was to make this work. That was to be hoped, of course. But if she was unwilling to commit to him voluntarily, she was going to have to be persuaded. The possibilities were endless.

Shannon accepted the prince's arm as it came around her, leading her into the dance, and she felt her traitorous body begin to respond to him again. It just didn't make any sense. She'd made up her mind that the man was abhorrent. Why couldn't the rest of her system get the message?

Still, she'd promised Greta to do something to make amends, and she supposed it was only fair that she do so. After tonight she would never see the crown prince again, but Greta and Freddy—and most of all the real princess—would have to deal with him on a continuing basis. Time to smooth feathers.

She took a deep breath and raised her eyes to meet his. "I want to apologize for some of the things I said to you earlier. I'm afraid I got a little carried away."

He nodded his head in acknowledgment. "That is very gracious of you, Princess," he said.

She waited, holding his gaze with her own, trying not to notice the attractive deep grooves that had once housed dimples in his handsome face, and definitely ignoring the full lips.

"Well?" she said at last.

He looked into her face and it was obvious he knew she was waiting for him to reciprocate. Was that a spark of humor in his silver-blue eyes? Or a flicker of malice?

"Well what?" he asked innocently.

Her own eyes flashed sparks. "Aren't *you* going to apologize to *me?*"

"Certainly. Once I've found something wrong with my behavior."

She stopped the gasp that started up her throat and pressed lips together. No, she wasn't going to let him do this to her again. She swallowed hard, forcing back anger. "That's all I ask," she said as sweetly as she could.

"All right," he said grudgingly, as though he'd decided he could at least give her this. "I know we got off on the wrong foot. I'm sure I said some things that would have been better left unsaid. So let's start anew."

She could tell that she wasn't going to get anything better from him. Nodding slightly, she gave him a thin smile. "Agreed."

"Good. That gives us an opportunity to discuss the situation we are in."

"The situation?"

The situation. She hoped she knew enough about it for discussion. But once again, she would have to be careful she didn't make any commitments for the princess. Keeping things general sounded like the best way to go. She glanced up at him, then looked away. She felt as though she were preparing for a pop quiz.

"Yes. The situation we both find ourselves in. I have no idea how you feel about it."

She hesitated. "Why don't you describe it to me the way you see it?" she said, stalling for time.

"It's simple enough. I owe your father for his support, both in manpower and in political arm-twisting, in freeing Nabotavia from the radicals. If it weren't for him, I probably wouldn't be going back." He turned his brilliant gaze on her. "He asked in return that I marry his beloved daughter. And I promised him I'd do it."

She studied his face, hoping to find one little kernel of human feeling somewhere in all that beautiful coolness. "That's it?"

"Yes. What more do you need?" He shrugged. "You have to admit, it is rather awkward for both of us."

She frowned, wanting to be sure she got this straight. "In other words, you don't really want to marry the princess."

He opened his mouth to answer, then frowned at the way she'd put that. "I have promised King Mandrake that I would offer his daughter my name and a place at my side in Nabotavia. And I mean to honor that promise."

She nodded, reminding herself not to slip into the third person again. "I see. I think I get it. So even though you don't really want to marry me, you're bound and determined to do it to pay back King Mandrake."

"No, you *don't* really get it." He looked pained. "That's why we need to talk this over."

She gave him a dubious look. "Yes, I can certainly see the need for some frank conversation."

"Very good. The sooner the better." He glanced over his shoulder. "Why don't we find a more private area and…"

"Oh no." She saw where this was going and she wasn't going to go there. He wanted time alone while he probed her mind for her real reactions to marrying him? What a recipe for complete disaster.

He blinked, looking down at her in surprise, as though he wasn't sure if he'd heard her right. "No?"

"No, I'm sorry, I can't do that."

She'd promised Greta she would repair the break and she felt she'd taken care of things on that score. Her obligations were fulfilled and she was going home. She sighed with relief as the dance came to an end. This time she wasn't waiting for anyone to fetch her and she slipped out of Marco's arms. Gathering a handful of skirt, she smiled at him.

"Thank you very much for a lovely evening. It's been most interesting. And now, I'll bid you good night."

And she turned and sped away, knowing she was leaving a very perplexed royal behind, but not really caring a bit.

Shannon was out in front of the hotel only a few minutes later, waiting for the limousine that would take her back to real life. She was still tingling from her encounter with the crown prince. She hoped never to see him again but the memory of all that masculine elegance would be a treasured one for a long time. A young woman like her—a graduate art history student paying her way through college as a hostess in a Texas steak house—didn't get too many opportunities to see royalty up close and personal.

"It's been fun," she murmured to herself, craning her neck to see if the limousine was coming, "but thank goodness it's over."

Greta and Freddy were lingering inside, saying goodbye to old friends and acquaintances, but Shannon was anxious to leave her semi-royal life behind. And somewhat nervous about getting away from the hotel before the prince showed up and tried to talk to her again.

A long, sleek limousine pulled up and a mournful-looking man stepped out, leaving the passenger side door open and indicating he'd done so for her convenience.

"If you please, Your Highness," he said, making a sweeping movement with his arm and bowing in her direction.

"Thank you," she said, bending to slip into the back seat, relieved that she was going to make her escape. Fussing with her long skirt, she didn't notice that the back seat was already occupied until she'd set herself down in the corner and looked up. And then, her gaze meeting the calm demeanor of the crown prince, she gasped. "You!"

She'd barely got the word out when the door slammed shut and the driver of the limousine began to cruise toward the highway.

"Princess," Marco said, bowing slightly from

where he sat. "I'm honored that you have agreed to join me in a ride to see the lights of the city."

She gaped at him, outraged. "I have done no such thing and you know it."

His gaunt, shadowed face showed no reaction. "We need to talk."

"*You* may need to talk. *I* need to get some sleep. Turn this thing around and take me back right now!"

His jaw tightened. "Iliana, be reasonable. We need to get some things settled between us."

She looked at him helplessly. She was stuck and she knew it. And all for nothing. She couldn't settle anything. She wasn't in the position to make promises. Or even to tell simple truths. He was going to ask all sorts of things she couldn't answer. Now what?

She made one last pathetic attempt to change his mind.

"I really can't go with you. I have a headache. I need to get home. And anyway, Greta and Freddy won't know what's happened to me." She looked back longingly toward the fading lights of the hotel where those two were still chatting with old friends.

"My man Jordan will stay behind and fill them in," the crown prince said reassuringly. "I'll make sure you get home in one piece."

Home! That was another problem. She couldn't let him drop her at the little house in the modest suburb where she actually lived. And if he took her out to the princess's ranch, it would be daybreak before she made her way home again.

She turned to look at him, dismayed. He was certainly making her life difficult. Her chin came up and her eyes flashed. "I insist that you turn this car around and take me back," she said, surprising herself with how imperious she sounded.

Her manner appeared to surprise him, too. He actually seemed to look at her for the first time and really see how upset she was.

"I'm sorry, Iliana," he said quietly. "I can't do that. We must talk and we don't have much time. This has got to be settled right away."

She stared at him and realized she was at a crossroads. She could throw a tantrum until he got so disgusted with her he dropped her on the closest street corner. Or she could tough it out, do what she could to avoid answering direct questions, and hope for the best. With a sigh, she opted for the latter.

"All right, Your Royal Highness," she said, settling back into the plush cushions. "Since I've been shanghaied, I guess I might as well make the best of it. Let's talk."

Chapter Three

Marco pulled open his tie, glancing at Princess Iliana. Now that he had her here, he could relax. He purposefully worked his shoulders, loosening them, releasing tension, and stretched his long legs out before him. His original reaction to the beautiful woman beside him had mellowed somewhat. She wasn't as bad as he'd insisted she was when he'd talked to Jordan, but she certainly had turned out to be very different from what he'd first expected.

But what had he expected exactly? Ever since he'd made the alliance with King Mandrake and agreed to marry his daughter, people had been whispering warnings in his ear. Or shouting them at full volume. He almost grinned, thinking of his mother-in-law, Lady Judith, who had been explicit.

"You can't marry that woman. She's a floozy."

The mother of his beloved wife Lorraine, Judith was still a major factor in his life as well as the main caretaker of his two young children. Her opinion mattered. Still, he was a man who believed in keeping his word. Breaking the promise he'd made to King Mandrake would threaten the stability of his newly freed country. His own personal happiness wasn't as important as the well-being of his country.

For just a moment a picture flashed into his mind. A small, slender pixie of a woman was dancing before him, her dark eyes warm with laughter, her short-cropped gamin hair hugging her head. "Catch me if you can, Mister Crown Prince," she teased him as she darted away, and his heart twisted with love for her.

His wife, Lorraine, had died almost two years before and the pain sometimes swept through him in a wave that choked and weakened. He pushed her memory away. He wasn't going to think of her. He couldn't allow himself the self-indulgence of it. He had to live in the here and now. He had a country to run. And he had to prepare to take a new wife, no matter how much that thought repelled him.

He'd forgotten the princess sat beside him until she said something and he turned toward her with a start, then realized she was asking for a drink of water. Nodding, he pulled an ice-cold bottle out of the little refrigerator and handed it to her, studying her quietly as he did so.

Iliana looked nothing like Lorraine. That was good. It was going to be difficult enough to avoid making comparisons as it was. He had to treat this as a whole new experience. Lorraine was a love match. This was…something else. The capacity for romantic love had died in him the day Lorraine was killed.

At the same time, he couldn't help but feel Judith was wrong. This woman was no floozy.

"Dallas is beautiful," he said, looking out at the sparkling lights set in the blackness of the night as the limousine cruised down the highway.

"Yes," she responded. "And it's even better when you can actually see it."

He almost smiled and he had to admit, that was progress. Her quips were beginning to seem more amusing than annoying. "Why did you pick Dallas, Iliana?" he asked.

"Why did I pick Dallas?" she echoed blankly, ready to bristle.

"What made you move here?"

"Oh." She avoided his gaze. What was the reason again? Greta had filled her in. *Oh yes.* "My father bought the ranch for me." She looked at him sideways. "He was hoping to interest me in settling down in a nice town where there was an established Alovitian community he would have ties to."

"And away from the bright lights of the big bad coastal cities?"

"Exactly."

"And did his ploy work?"

"Well...." She frowned. This weaving in and out of what she could actually say was getting tiring fast. "I have to say I do love Dallas," she said quickly instead of answering. "I've been very happy here."

She looked into his eyes, noting the intelligence that shone from them, but also the moody restlessness that seemed to lurk in the dark shadows. As she was calming down and taking this conversation as the currently necessary evil that it was, she was losing some of her animosity toward him. He was still high-handed and arrogant—but hey, he was a crown prince. That was part of his role in life, she supposed. She just had to remember that she was a princess and therefore didn't need to give way to him entirely.

She tried to put herself in his position. Here he was, talking to the woman he had arranged to marry, trying to find out…what? What could she tell him that would put his mind at ease and make him stop asking her questions she could never hope to answer? In his next statement, he told her.

"What I really want to do is to get to know you better."

She reacted with a short laugh. This was exactly what she wanted to avoid. "Oh no. Getting to know me tonight is not a good idea."

"Why not?"

"I'm just…well, I'm not myself tonight." *Oh very cute, Shannon!* She bit her lip and looked at him quickly, bracing to hear him say something cutting. But he looked closer to a smile than a sneer, and he responded calmly.

"I realize you have amnesia for anything that happened before you turned twenty-one. But how about what happened after? Fill me in."

She swallowed and looked out the window. The Dallas skyline was etched across a purple-black sky in spears of glittering lights. What in the world could she tell him?

"From what I've heard, you did attend university for a time," he prompted.

She turned back to him, pathetically grateful for a

subject she could discuss. "Oh yes. I did attend the Sorbonne." Greta *had* said that, hadn't she?

"Ah." He looked interested. "I've been accused of being overly academic myself at times. You, too?"

The princess? Hardly. But Shannon herself was another matter and she couldn't resist reacting. "Oh, I love learning new things. Especially history and science and art. Everything new I learn seems to put the pieces of this giant puzzle the world can be into a more understandable order. Do you know what I mean?"

"I do." He actually looked pleased. "What was your major field of study at the Sorbonne?"

Her heart jumped. What in the world had they said she had studied? She couldn't remember. It was something like French or Norwegian or some other language. Better not to risk an answer. Instead, she shook her head and smiled at him brightly, counting on charm to get her through.

"Oh that was so long ago. Let's not talk about that." As she realized she needed to think of something else to talk about fast, her smile got so bright her cheeks began to ache. "How about you? Where did you go to school?"

His expression had warmed, but she was afraid that was mostly because he was about to laugh out loud at the ridiculous picture she made with her pasted-on grin.

"We'll get to that," he told her, his smoky eyes unreadable. "Right now I want to find out all I can about you. Tell me, what are your interests?"

"Oh…uh…" What could she say? What had she heard? Drinking and gambling in Las Vegas would not be a good answer here. Ah, but there was something else.

"Riding!" That was a safe bet. Why would her father have bought the horse ranch for her if she didn't like horses? "Yes, I love riding. I do it all the time."

"Really? Do you use a Western or an English style saddle?"

"Uh…both."

"Both?"

Bad answer? She was no expert but it didn't seem so wacky to her. "Sure. Whichever fits my mood at the time."

The skeptical look he gave her made her anxious for only a moment. Getting a reputation for smart-aleck remarks was holding her in good stead. It looked like he was taking any statement she made that was in any way ridiculous as though it were a joke. She gave a small sigh of relief. Saved again.

"Living at a Texas ranch must seem very different from the atmosphere you grew up in near Paris," he mentioned.

She nodded. She'd been to the ranch. In fact, that was where she'd been schooled by Greta and Freddy when she was first hired. It also often served as the base of operation for the various outings to charity events. So she knew that it was a working ranch with many employees and a horse breeding program.

"We're training horses there, you know," she told him. "I'm sure you'll be interested in seeing the whole setup if you come back next month."

"Undoubtedly."

She noticed his slightly raised eyebrow at her use

of the word *if*, but she didn't retract it. After all, this was still a job interview. He was trying to decide if it was worth his time to come back, wasn't he?

The funny thing was, the animosity that had flared between them so hotly at the ball seemed to have melted away. There was still an edginess there, but the outright hostility was gone. That was a relief, she supposed. After all, it would have been unfair to leave things the way they had been and let the real princess walk into a minefield.

On the other hand, it was probably more dangerous for Shannon herself.

He looked out the window at the passing night-scape and then turned back. "Aren't you going to point out some of the more notable landmarks for me?" he asked.

"Sure." She leaned closer so that she could see what he was seeing and began to name buildings and areas of the city. It occurred to her halfway through her recitation that she was showing off a lot of knowledge for someone who had only lived here for a few months. But once she was launched, it was hard to stop. She really did love this place and she was proud of it.

"And there is the Roundup Steak Corral," she said, risking a secret smile as she pointed out the restaurant where she worked part-time as a hostess as they rolled past it. "Best steaks in Texas."

Despite its name and the neon picture of a bucking bronco over its entrance, the place was a high-end steakhouse, popular with tourists from the luxury hotels that surrounded it, as well as with local businessmen. Marco looked at it, then turned and gave her a questioning look.

"Uh-huh," he said dubiously.

Laughing softly, she realized she was closer to him now than she'd been since they'd danced together and that old black magic was working again. Awareness was seeping into her blood and rising lazily through her body. She knew it was time to pull back and sit on the opposite side of the limousine again, but it took her a moment to make herself do it. In one last long glance she took in his thick dark eyelashes and the way tiny hairs curled at his hairline. And as her blood began to pump with a new urgency through her veins, she drew back regretfully.

She'd warmed to him. That was obvious. And he was acting very civilly to her. But she didn't try to fool herself. She knew he was just as cool and judgmental underneath as he had been from the beginning. After all, he was looking over a prospective wife the same way a rancher looked over a new thoroughbred he was contemplating adding to his herd.

That thought made her frown.

"May I offer you some champagne?" he asked, displaying a large bottle.

She shook her head. "No thank you. I don't drink."

"You don't drink?" He looked at her in surprise.

Oh-oh. Her radar went up. This could be a problem. The princess probably drank like a fish. "No, uh, I don't. At least for tonight."

"At least for tonight?" he repeated, staring at her as though she were a space traveler who had suddenly dropped into his limousine. "I see."

Her shoulders sagged. This was impossible. How could she sustain this playacting in any credible way? She was tempted to turn to him right now and tell him the truth. Sneaking a look at him sideways, she wondered what he would do if she came right out with it.

Listen, Prince, I can't keep lying to you. I'm not the princess at all. I'm just playing her for the time being, while she is off doing whatever princesses do when they are being naughty and defying their fathers. Can I go home now?

She looked at him speculatively, noticing again the hard line to his jaw, the flash of ice in his gaze, and she shivered, deciding against it. She might as well go to plan B and try to get him talking about something other than the fascinating nuances of Iliana's madcap life.

"Now you tell me about yourself," she said, hoping to steer the conversation into areas where she wouldn't have to weigh every word before she uttered it. "What have you been doing?"

"The usual things." His shrug was elegantly casual. "Oxford, then post-grad work in government and political science. Attending international conferences, internships of sorts with various heads of state, gathering support for taking back Nabotavia, then the liberation fight last year."

"That's it?" she said when he'd finished, turning her hands palms up. "You're done?"

"Well, those are the highlights."

She gazed at him quizzically. "More like an outline of the highlights. Phoned in from beyond the horizon."

She might have been mistaken, but she thought she really saw a spark of humor in his gaze.

"Sorry," he said gruffly. "But I've never been particularly chatty."

"Nor one to overstate the obvious," she said with a quick smile.

He almost smiled back but he caught himself in time. This princess was surprising him at every turn. So far, she seemed to be at least three different people. There was the bad girl he'd known ten years ago who'd become the coquette everyone had warned him about, the annoying challenger he'd recently danced with…and now this vibrant sunny personality that appealed to him in ways he wasn't sure he was comfortable with.

"Which is it, Iliana?" he wanted to ask her. "Will the real princess please step forward?"

And then he frowned, recapturing his usual serious tone, and changed the subject.

"Tell me this, Princess. What are your feelings for Nabotavia? Can you picture yourself her queen?"

"Oh yes." Now on this one she could expand and tell the truth at the same time. "I love Nabotavia. At least, all I know of her. I've never actually been there, of course."

His face showed no reaction to her declaration. "Your father has contacted you about this, hasn't he?"

"Yes, certainly." *That* she knew for sure. Contacted and recontacted. And all the while, there were Greta and Freddy, afraid to tell King Mandrake that his daughter had skipped town with her boyfriend.

"Iliana, if you are dead set against this marriage, tell me now so I know what I'm dealing with."

She turned her bright violet gaze on him, hesitated, then rushed out a disclaimer. "You know, we weren't expecting you until next month. So I haven't really thought this through the way I will need to."

He stared at her, searching her face, and she wished she could look away.

"I'm sure you know there are many rumors about what you've been up to for the last few years."

She nodded, feeling as miserable as if she really were the one the rumors were about.

"I don't want to know any details. The only thing I need to know is if there is anything that could hurt my children or bring shame to the people of Nabotavia."

She was silent for a moment, staring at the folded hands in her lap, wondering how on earth she could deal with this. "That is a very good question," she said slowly at last. "It deserves a well-thought-out answer." She gave him a dazzling smile to cover up her inner unease. "I'm sorry, Marco, but I really can't give you a definitive answer today."

He nodded slowly. "I understand. And I appreciate the seriousness you're taking this with."

That cut like a knife. If he ever realized the hoax she was perpetrating, he wouldn't be able to appreciate anything about her ever again. But what did it matter? He was leaving first thing in the morning and she was quitting this job last thing tonight.

And then, as though a switch was thrown in her mind, it occurred to her that she was sitting right next to the crown prince of the nation she loved best, next to her own. His was the country she was studying. He was a fabulous resource and she had only this short time with him. She was never going to have another chance like this. She couldn't let it pass her by. Thinking quickly, she tried to put her finger on something that would be new and different.

"You know what?" she said, trying to leash her eagerness. "I would love to hear about some of your experiences during the war of liberation for Nabotavia. Did you get wounded?"

A flicker of surprise lit his blue eyes. "Not really."

"Did you take pictures?"

He looked at her as though he weren't sure if she were serious. "Iliana. It was a war."

"People take pictures of war. You should get your reminiscences down on paper, you know. Hire someone to write a book about them. Make a movie." The idea appealed to her. Now she was getting really excited. "Yes! You're going to be king, you can hire people to do these things. Nabotavia will want a movie about its independence." She frowned, thinking hard. "Who could we get to play you?"

"Iliana…" He laughed.

She stared at him, realizing this was the first time she'd seen real happy humor on his lean face. It was pretty darn spectacular and it set her back on her heels, reminding her that she couldn't get too close to him.

She went on a bit more carefully, asking him questions and getting him to open up a bit about how the liberation of Nabotavia had been staged. Reluctant at first, he began to get into the telling of the story and soon he was giving her anecdotes he probably hadn't repeated to another human being. But when he realized it, she could see him begin to close down again, looking restless.

"I'm getting tired of riding around the city in this limousine," he said at last. "Is there a nice river where we could take a walk?"

"A river?" She laughed aloud. "Mister, you're in the middle of Texas. But if you want to go for a walk, I know a very nice, well-lit park with a man-made lake. And it's only a few blocks from here."

A word to the driver and they were there.

"Let's go over there by the water," Marco suggested.

Couples were walking along the water's edge and benches were set haphazardly among the trees. They found an empty one and sat where they could watch the passing scene but be far enough from it for private conversation.

"I'm really going to have to get home soon," she said, looking at him sideways and then looking out at the water again.

"So soon?"

"I have to work...I mean, I've got somewhere I have to be tomorrow. I've got to get some sleep or I'll be worthless."

"I won't keep you much longer," he promised.

"What do you still want to talk about?" she asked him, turning toward him on the bench, but looking somehow guarded in a way that reminded him of the way she'd seemed earlier that evening.

He thought for a moment, wondering if this was really the right time for this. He would feel so much more comfortable with a decision about a battle plan or an economic move. Human relations were not his forte. Still, he felt he needed to fill her in on the situation she would be entering when they married. It was only fair.

"You do know that I was married before," he said at last, charging ahead now that he'd decided to do it.

She nodded, staring away from him.

"My wife, Lorraine, was killed in an automobile accident outside of Paris two years ago."

She turned back, looking at him, her eyes filled with sudden compassion that he hadn't expected.

"Oh, I'm so sorry!"

He blinked. Surely she already knew all this. He was just going over it to touch bases and remind her of how it was. He'd planned a quick dispassionate background story but her reaction, the sympathy in her huge violet eyes, opened a door to an emotion he hadn't planned to express and suddenly he found himself saying more.

"She left me with two little children…and a shattered heart." Funny, he'd never put it in just those words to anyone before. But it was true and it seemed right to tell her this way. "She was my life and when she died, a part of me was gone."

He cleared his throat, surprised to find it closing. Shaking that away, he tried to keep his voice cool and steady. "I just wanted to make sure you to understood…how I feel. But I need a wife, my children need a mother, and my country needs a queen."

"You really loved her, didn't you?" she said softly, her gaze searching his as though to find some of his pain and help him with it.

"I still love her," he said, his voice husky with the emotion he had been trying to keep at bay. "We fell in love as children and continued to grow closer as adults. She was the best thing that ever happened to me."

He was the one turning away now, but she put a hand on his sleeve as though to keep him there.

"Please. Tell me what she was like."

He took a deep breath. No one had ever asked him that before. Half closing his eyes, he saw her again as she used to be.

"She was very small and very beautiful, and she had the energy of a hummingbird." A sad smile tilted his lips. "She reminded me of a forest sprite. Where other people walked, she danced. When she wasn't talking, she was singing. Her laughter filled our home with light." His voice got stronger as he recalled the good things and he turned back to look at the woman beside him. "Her joy in life was a direct counterpoint to my more serious outlook. We complemented each other. Together, we formed a whole person. Without her," he added, wincing slightly, "I'm only half alive."

Shannon's eyes filled with tears. She tried to see his face but everything was shimmering. She wanted to study his features so that she would always be able to see his face the way it was when he had uttered these touching words. If only someday someone would love *her* this way.

"I didn't realize you had two children," she murmured, almost to herself. "No one told me that."

Slowly it dawned on her that she was doing a terrible thing. This wasn't right. She shouldn't be hearing this. The real Iliana should hear it. It might very well change how she felt about him. It might change a lot of things. And he might never tell her, thinking he already had. This was wrong. She was treading in areas where she had no right to be. She was going to have to do something to make this right, but she didn't have time to mull over what that might be, because he had his emotions under control again and was rising from the bench, taking her by the hand.

"You still haven't given me any hint as to how you feel about our situation," he said. "If you have any misgivings, it would be better to get them into the open now."

"I'm sorry, Marco," she said earnestly. "You'll just have to wait. I'm not ready to make a commitment. I'm sure I'll be ready when you come back to Dallas…"

He shrugged. "I've changed my plans. I've decided to stay for a few more days. I'm sure we'll see a lot of each other." His jaw hardened. "But I want you to understand that I'm determined to marry you. And I want to have your promise by the time I leave."

"I understand," she said, wishing she didn't have to be so noncommittal. He deserved better.

She had to admit it—she liked him. She hadn't meant to like him. She'd never wanted to like him. Since she was never going to see him again, it hardly made any difference if she liked him. But still, there it was.

Soon he would be married to the princess, a woman she'd never met. She'd defended her earlier, but now that she knew the prince better, she felt defensive for *him.* She was afraid he wasn't getting a fair deal in this bargain. But there really wasn't anything she could do about it.

His cell phone rang and he pulled it out of his pocket, flipping it open to answer the call. "All right," he said. "We'll be back in a few minutes."

Closing the phone, he grinned at her. "It seems your Freddy and Greta are quite the worrywarts. They are still at the hotel waiting for you."

"What?"

"They have your limousine waiting and insist I drop you back there so that they can take you home themselves."

Oh. Of course. And a good thing, too.

"Well, they do get very nervous about me," she said apologetically. "Perhaps it would be best to humor them."

"I have a couple of business meetings tomorrow morning," he said as they walked. "And a business lunch. But I'll come out to your ranch in the evening, if that is convenient for you."

She didn't know what to say. Maybe Greta and Freddy would be able to contact the real princess by then. In any case, she wouldn't be there. A knot of sadness was forming just below her rib cage. She felt like Cinderella, racing against the clock. But leaving a slipper behind wouldn't do any good. She was never going to see Crown Prince Marco again, no matter how many clues she left.

Chapter Four

Shannon made it to work the next morning only five minutes late. That gave her quite a sense of accomplishment, considering she'd slipped into bed at four in the morning, then lain awake for hours replaying the amazing evening she'd had, and finally fell asleep as the sun began peeking in her window.

Dragging herself back out of bed at what she'd thought was nine, she'd suddenly realized it was actually ten. She'd barely had time to take a shower and get dressed for work before dashing off toward the Turtle Creek area near the Roundup Steak Corral.

She had on her Annie Oakley costume, just like everyone who worked there wore, with the felt hat, complete with fake auburn curls, and the tooled cowboy boots and the gun belt on her hips. Unfortunately there were no guns in the holsters, not even play guns. The political correctness police had convinced management that even historical representations of firearms were a bad influence on children and they had been banned. She felt a little silly wearing the empty holsters. But then, the entire outfit usually put a grin on the face of anyone who hadn't been to the steakhouse before.

"It just says 'Texas' to out-of-towners," Randy, the restaurant manager told her when she'd complained that it made her feel ridiculous. "People love it. And you look darn cute in it, honey."

That made her back away. Randy had never actually made a move on her, but he leered a lot and she was wary.

"Well, look at this," he said today, coming around the corner as she clocked in. "Gina's already working. I've got two hostesses in when I only need one. Someone goofed up the scheduling again."

She turned to look at the big beefy man.

"If you need a volunteer to go home, I'm your gal," she told him, stifling a yawn.

He frowned at her. "You've been missing all sorts of hours lately."

She gave him a guilty smile. "I've been doing something important, but that's all over now."

He nodded slowly, considering. "Tell you what. I'll let Gina be hostess today, but I need you to help with an important lunch party coming in soon. They've reserved the small banquet room for a business lunch. When they're done, you can go home."

Shannon sighed. He was asking her to waitress. She'd worked her way up to hostess and she hated to backtrack, but he was right. She did need the hours.

"Okay," she told him. "I'll help with the banquet."

She went into the banquet room to help Janice, a waitress, and Todd, the busboy, set up, chatting about inconsequential things as she began laying out the silverware in the place settings. When she turned back to get the napkins, she saw that someone had put the morning paper on the counter, front page up, and she glanced at it, then did a double take. There she was just under the fold, with the headline, Crown Prince Finds His Princess At Local Ball. She grabbed the paper, then glanced at the other two to see if they had noticed. Her heart was thumping in her chest. There she was, dancing with Marco, looking up at him adoringly. Had she really looked at him that way? Impossible. But there it was in living color.

She hadn't noticed anyone taking pictures. She hadn't noticed any press covering it at all. But someone must have been. Because there they were. Not that anyone she knew would realize it was her. It didn't look like the Shannon Harper anyone outside of royal circles knew. And that in itself was so crazy.

She'd been very successfully keeping her mind on other things ever since she'd jumped out of bed an hour late that morning, but now it all came flooding back to her and she turned the paper facedown, trying to shove it away again.

"A magic knight," said the caption to the picture, making an obvious play on words. But that was exactly what Marco looked like. Had it been a "magic night," as well? Not exactly. "More like a nightmare," she grumbled to herself, but she knew she was bluffing. The night before had been like nothing else in her life had ever been or would ever be. Because of that, it would always be special to her. But she wished it weren't on the cover of the newspaper.

She was finished with the princess business. All that remained was for her to run out to the ranch and pick up her things, which she planned to do that afternoon. Then she would cut all ties to the royals and their shenanigans forever.

"The banquet party is starting to arrive," Todd announced, rushing to fill the water glasses.

"Okay," Shannon said, her back to the entrance as she stood across the room gathering the extra pieces of silverware together and putting them away behind the service station.

She heard two men entering, talking in low tones, and suddenly she froze when she heard a familiar voice.

"I was told on the highest authority that this place has the best steaks in Dallas."

Her heart stopped. No! It couldn't be. She gripped the edge of the table where she stood, not daring to turn around. Oh please, make it be some man who has exactly the same voice as Crown Prince Marco. Please, please, please!

"I've got to tell you some of the boys groused when I changed the restaurant on them at the last minute," another voice said. "Especially the vegetarians."

"Oh, we have a vegetarian entrée," Janice told them quickly. "And some wonderful salads. I'm sure your friends will be pleased."

"I'm sure they will be, too," the voice that sounded like Marco said. "But I'm going to order the biggest steak you've got."

Scraping chairs. They were being seated. She was going to have to turn around and greet them. She was stuck unless she wanted to try sidling out like a crab with her face to the wall. She was going to have to turn and look at him. She glanced into the mirror along the sideboard. She did look different. The red curls helped. Maybe he wouldn't even notice.

Silently, she counted to ten, took a deep breath, and turned.

It was him all right. He hadn't looked at her yet. Maybe she could just slip around him and…

He turned and looked directly into her face, his eyes widening with astonishment. So much for the forlorn hope that he wouldn't notice her. Shannon put on her sassiest smile. It was do-or-die time.

"Hi there," she said in her most robust Texas drawl. "How y'all doin?" She smiled down at Marco. "Mister, can I rustle you up somethin' to drink while you're waitin' on your friends?"

"Iliana?" he said in disbelief, searching her face.

"Who?" she asked him, eyes wide and innocent.

"Iliana, what…"

"Sorry, mister," she said, shaking her head as though she hadn't a clue what he was talking about. "I think you've got me mixed up with someone else." She pointed to the nameplate pinned above her pocket. "My name's Shannon. Now tell me what I can get you to drink, why don't you?"

He blinked, leaning back in his chair. "Iced tea," he murmured, looking stunned and doubtful.

"Fruit-flavored or regular?"

"Regular, please."

"Sure thing. And how 'bout you?" she asked his companion.

"What have you got on tap?" he asked.

She went through the litany she knew by heart automatically, her mind on Marco. He was staring at her in bewilderment. She could see him out of the corner of her eye. He wasn't sure whether to believe her. He was wondering if he were hallucinating. And he was getting more angry about the whole situation by the second. That much she could tell by the vibes he was sending her way. She had to get out of here.

"Thank you, gentlemen," she said, finishing up the order. "I'll have your drinks back for you in no time at all."

No time at all. That was the truth of it. She hurried from the room and slapped the order form down on the bar, trying to think.

"Hey, Shannon, what's with the fake accent?" Todd asked, grinning as he followed her out of the banquet room.

She shook her head and flashed him a look. "Don't ask. I'll fill you in later."

Randy came into the bar area and she appealed to him. "Randy, I've got an emergency. I have to go."

"What?" His face reddened. "You can't go. I need you here." He frowned angrily. "Listen, I've given you enough second chances, Shannon. You go now and I don't want you coming back."

She gulped in air. No time to argue. Instead on answering him, she headed in the general direction of the kitchen, but veered off into the locker room once she got around the corner. She had to get out of this crazy getup and get out of here. She knew it was only a matter of minutes before Marco would begin to realize she wasn't coming back into that room. Once he saw that, he would begin to think maybe he'd been right when he'd called her Iliana. Then he would start going through the restaurant, looking for her. She didn't have much time. Luckily she had a change of clothes in her locker. Now if she could only get out of here before Randy noticed.

Time for this Texas Cinderella to grab her pumpkin and split.

Moments later she was in her little economy car, racing toward the princess's ranch. She'd changed into jeans and a cropped pink jersey shirt and let her long hair down. She was all Shannon Harper now. Not the princess. Not even the steakhouse waitress. She was going to grab all the things she'd left out at the ranch and head for home before Marco had time to put two and two together. There would be no trace of her then. He'd never find her—unless Greta and Freddy talked. But why would they? From the way they'd acted right from the beginning she knew they probably had a lot more to lose than she did if this whole facade fell apart. After all, they'd been lying to King Mandrake, too afraid to let him know his daughter wasn't following his wishes. She was only losing a part time job, they were risking losing their life's work and status, as she understood it. So it would probably be best to warn them if they were available.

Flipping open her cell phone, she carefully negotiated punching in their number while her car careened way over the speed limit down the long empty highway. The number rang and rang, and finally a voice answered.

"Hello?"

"Rosa?" She recognized the voice of the house-keeper. "Hi. It's Shannon. Is Greta there?"

"No, she's not here."

"How about Freddy?"

"He's gone, too."

"Where did they go?"

"*No sé.* They don't tell me. But they go very fast. Like the devil was coming to get them."

"Oh, darn. Listen, can you do me a favor? Please get my backpack with my textbooks and my makeup kit out of the pink bedroom and have them ready for me to pick up? I'm heading your way. I should be there in about fifteen minutes. I just want to grab my things and go. Can you do that?"

"Sure."

"And Rosa…please don't tell anyone I'm coming out there. Okay? Especially anyone who phones."

"*Bueno.*"

"Thanks so much, Rosa. I'll be seeing you in a few minutes."

Her heart was beating hard, adrenaline pumping—she had to admit this was sort of exciting. *Just as long as I don't get caught!*

She wondered what Marco was doing right now. He had looked so handsome. She had to admit, much as he'd panicked her, she hadn't minded seeing him again. If only there wasn't this awful lie between them. It would be so much fun to actually show him the city as her own true self, take him line dancing, maybe. Or to a real Texas barbecue. But that was a silly thought. The lie was in the way, and if it weren't for the lie, she wouldn't have ever met him.

She could see him asking Janice what had happened to the other waitress, then when Janice told him she didn't know, perhaps going to find Randy and asking again. By that time, someone would have noticed her uniform on the floor of the locker room where she'd left it, and Randy would be fuming. What would happen next? What would Marco say to Randy?

"This waitress, Shannon something. How long has she worked here?"

And Randy would say, "Shannon? Oh let's see. I know she's been with us since before she graduated college because we had a little party for her when she got her degree. She's been working here part-time for most of the last four years. And before that, her mother was our bookkeeper. Why do you ask?"

And then Marco would know that either he was crazy or this Shannon person was a look-alike like no other. But why had she skipped out after seeing him? Very fishy behavior.

So what would he do then? Call the ranch, she would bet, trying to get hold of Iliana, or at least Greta and Freddy. And all he would get would be Rosa. He would ask for directions to the ranch and maybe call for the limousine to take him out there, but by that time she would be long gone.

And once he got to the ranch, what would he be told? She didn't have any control over that. Leave it to Greta and Freddy. They were very good at making up stories. Let them try to explain it.

Still, she couldn't help but feel a touch of sadness.

She would probably never see him again, except in pictures and maybe on television. She hardly knew him, and yet somehow, that seemed an awful waste. Something told her they might have been good friends under other circumstances. Good friends, or maybe even... She shook her head. That didn't bear speculating about. Not yet. Not until she was safely away. She saw the ranch ahead with its rolling pastures and long white fences. Tall cottonwoods lined the long driveway up to the white ranch house, their green leaves flickering in the Texas sun. She skidded to a stop right in front of the big double doors, jumped out of the car and raced inside, leaving the engine still running.

"Thanks, Rosa," she called out as she grabbed her things, which had been stacked in the foyer, and turned back to put them into her car. Before she'd reached the exit she heard a car door slam. She gasped, but then realized it couldn't be him and kept going. He hadn't had time to get here. She had driven much too fast herself and besides, he wouldn't know how to get here until someone told him the directions, so...

There was no point in going on because he was striding toward the entrance. Her heart leaped into her throat. Could she make it to her car? One look into his cold hard face and she knew he would block her path. She hesitated, standing at the edge of the porch, her backpack and makeup case in her arms.

Marco gave her a look, then stopped by the open window of her car, reached in and switched off her engine, pulling out her keys as he did so. He tossed them into the air, caught them, and gently slipped them into the pocket of his suit coat. Then he came to the bottom of the steps and looked up at her, his hair tousled by the wind, his shirt open at the neck displaying tanned skin and a muscular chest. He looked very, very handsome and very, very angry.

"You want to tell me what the hell is going on?" he said, ripping off the dark glasses he wore and staring up at her.

"Oh. Hello." She tried to smile but she wasn't sure it came off looking like anything friendly. "What are you doing here?"

For one tiny moment she wondered if she could pull this off. Could she pretend to be the princess, pretend to have no idea who this Shannon Harper working at a steakhouse might be? Her mind raced as she stared into his silver-blue gaze.

But the jig was up. There were no more cards to play. And even if there had been a chance to get away with it, just looking into his angry eyes made her aware of how hopeless it would be for her to try to fool him. It had been one thing to lie when he'd been a stranger. He was something very different now. She knew him and felt a strange and slightly scary connection to him. It would be impossible to ever lie to him again.

She'd already decided she couldn't do it when the sound of a horse caught their attention and they both turned to see a handsome cowboy riding toward them from the stable area on a big beautiful pinto.

"Hey, Shannon," the cowboy said, his gaze flickering over Marco and then meeting hers with a question in it. "How's it goin'?"

"Hi, Jody," she said, swallowing. Jody was an old

friend from high school who had started working as a wrangler at the ranch just the week before. She'd seen him then and they'd had a nice long talk about the old days. She'd told him she was doing some research work for Greta. She didn't think he or any of the other regular ranch workers had any idea she was pretending to be the princess. But he'd obviously seen her drive up, and then saw Marco come dashing in behind her, and he decided to mosey on by and make sure she didn't need any help. "I'm just fine."

He nodded. "Nice to see you."

"You, too."

Jody looked at Marco coolly, tipping his hat before he wheeled the big pinto around and headed back for the corral. Marco barely gave him a glance. His fury was becoming more and more evident. His hands weren't clenched into fists, but they looked ready to do some sort of damage if the chance came up, and the pulse at his temple was throbbing like a train signal.

"You're not the princess."

He stated it as fact, but seemed almost as puzzled as he was angry, as though it was just starting to sink in that she really couldn't be whom she'd been presented as.

But the enormity of the situation was just beginning to hit her fully. She hated to face him this way. Suddenly she realized how very much she wanted his good opinion. And here she was, quickly losing it. Her shoulders sagged and she felt a little faint, but she didn't lower her gaze.

"That's right," she said firmly. "I'm not."

He started to speak, then just stood there shaking

his head, staring at her. "Who do I get to kill for coming up with this insane joke?" he said at last, his voice like ground glass.

She tried to smile but her facial muscles just weren't cooperating today. "I don't think this is quite a killing offense."

"Oh yeah? I'll make that decision when I know who did it."

He hadn't done anything, hadn't taken another step closer, but the sense of anger and danger that radiated from him was coming through loud and clear. Dropping her backpack to the ground, she reached out to prop herself against the railing. She really needed to sit down. Confronting the truth and the prince all at once was taking a bigger toll on her system than she'd expected.

Evaluating the situation at a glance, Marco moved quickly, coming up the steps and putting an arm around her.

"Let's go inside," he said gruffly. "That should be a better place to talk."

She held herself stiffly but allowed him to lead her back into the house. He felt hard and strong and very seductive as he led her into the living room. Why that should be she couldn't tell. It didn't make any sense. Here he was so angry with her he could explode and she was thinking about how sexy he was. Maybe there was a fatal flaw in her character. Or maybe there was a fatal gene all women carried that made them susceptible to insanity where attractive men were concerned. That had to be it, because she couldn't think of any other explanation for the way just touching him made her tremble.

Still, she managed to hide it while he helped her onto the couch, then faced her, dropping down to sit on the heavy coffee table.

"Are you all right?" he asked perfunctorily, studying her seriously.

"I'm fine," she said, holding her head high. She was not going to let him intimidate her.

"Okay then," he said. "Let's have it."

Where to begin? She looked at him helplessly. Rosa peeked around the corner, made a face at her and withdrew silently. Shannon only wished she could do the same.

"Start with this," he ordered. "Who are you and why do you look so much like Princess Iliana?"

She drew breath deep into her lungs and sat up even straighter. "My name is Shannon Harper. The way I look is just coincidence and luck, I guess. But because of it, I was hired to play the princess."

"In order to fool me?" he demanded scathingly, the veins in his neck standing out in a menacing way.

"No. Oh no." She hurried to reassure him, wishing she knew how to make him believe it. She wanted to reach out and touch him, maybe just on the arm, as evidence of her sincerity, but she resisted the impulse. He might think she was being too forward. "It wasn't about you at all. Not at first."

"Go on," he said, not looking reassured.

"Well, you see…" She paused, biting her lip. "Okay, let me start at the beginning. When Iliana's father bought her this ranch, he thought it would help…settle her." She snuck a look into his eyes, wondering how much he really knew about his intended and her wayward ways. "But she just couldn't stay put. Greta and Freddy were sent by the king to make sure she toed the line. They got her committed to all sorts of charity events, luncheons, supermarket openings…you know the drill.''

He nodded but his gaze was coolly pinning her to her seat.

''So she took off to parts unknown,'' she went on more quickly. ''And here they were with all these commitments and no princess. But since Iliana hadn't been here long, no one really knew her, so they got this idea to find someone who looked like her to do the personal appearances, so as not to disappoint people. And anyway, it was important for public relations. Or so they told me.''

That throbbing at his temple hadn't faded. In many ways, she had to marvel at how well he was keeping his temper leashed. With the anger she could see boiling in him she would expect more snarls, bulging eyes, a little knickknack smashing. Instead, he sat like a tightly coiled snake, all pulsing muscle that could do real damage if released, but still in control. She felt a slight shiver steal its way down her backbone. He really was a magnificent man.

''How long has this been going on?'' he asked, searching her eyes for answers.

She blinked, trying to hide them. ''Almost two months.'' She licked her dry and chapped lips. ''But I quit. I gave my notice last week. And I'm not doing it anymore.''

His head went back and he stared at her with those beautiful blue eyes. ''What about last night?''

''Last night.'' She cleared her throat and stared out the window. ''Yes, well… I really didn't want to do that, but Greta assured me we would meet, say a few words, and then we would part and that would be it.'' She threw one hand in the air. ''No one told me there would be dancing.''

''You attended a ball and didn't expect dancing?'' he asked her dryly. ''Interesting.''

She flushed.

''So you're just a hired look-alike.''

She spread out her palms. ''That's all I am.''

His raised eyebrow gave him a devilish air. ''Damn. I guess that means I'm not going to get to wring your neck.''

She nodded quickly. ''That's what it means all right.''

He stared at her for a long moment, studying her. ''Why did you take this job, Shannon Harper?'' he asked at last.

She shrugged. ''I needed the money.''

''Don't you already have a job at the steakhouse?''

''Yes. That's my bread-and-butter job. I'm working on a Master's degree in art history and that's the job that's putting me through school. But I have some unpaid bills I need to take care of. From when my mother died. She was very ill for a while and I'm still paying off those debts.''

He gazed at her with a speculative gleam in his eye and she sat very still, fighting the impulse to squirm. What was he thinking? She knew he despised her now. And why shouldn't he? He had every right to. Nobody liked to be tricked, but a crown prince had more than his personal dignity at stake. He was head of state of a country trying to come out of years of repression. From the little she knew of him she was sure he took that leadership very seriously. Suddenly she felt miserable. She hated being the one who had put him in this position.

"Tell me this," he said frostily. "Where is the princess right now?"

She shrugged. "I have no idea. The last I heard, she was supposedly in Las Vegas. But Greta hired detectives to find her, especially when she heard you were coming to the ball, and they came up empty."

He stared right through her for a moment. Reaching into the pocket of his suit coat, he pulled out a cell phone and flipped it open, poking out a number and putting it to his ear. "Jordan. I've got a job for you." Rising he went toward the window and she could only hear snatches of the conversation, though she could tell he was getting his man to hire someone to look for Iliana. Something told her he would have better luck than the others had. There was an air of certainty about him, an efficiency and cool intelligence that inspired confidence. And a bit of concern.

Biting her lip, she sighed softly. Regrets were beginning to rise out of the tight little place she'd been trying to keep them in, down in the depths of her heart. It had all seemed such a lark to pretend to be a princess and make a little money doing it. These unpleasant consequences hadn't occurred to her when she'd begun. She was sorry now, but it was a little late. She couldn't change what had been done.

Rising, she grabbed her purse and looked toward the door.

He noticed immediately, turning toward her. "Where are you going?"

She made a gesture toward where her car was

parked. "I've got to get back to town. I've got my seminar in post-modernism at four o'clock."

"Ah," he said, closing his phone and strolling back to where she stood. "At the University of Texas?"

"Yes."

His dark blue eyes seemed to smolder. "I suppose you've never actually attended the Sorbonne."

She tried to smile. "No."

His eyes narrowed. "So our entire evening, every conversation, was smoke and mirrors."

She swallowed, not sure why this seemed to matter to him. "Iliana *has* attended the Sorbonne. I was trying to give you answers that she might have given you, as near as I could figure."

He shook his head slowly, still holding her with his hard gaze. "Do you know Iliana?"

"No," she admitted, feeling like a criminal.

"You've never actually met her?"

"No."

That vein was throbbing at his temple again. "Did it ever occur to you three jolly pranksters that you were perpetrating a fraud? You can go to jail for that, you know."

"But we didn't harm anyone." Her heart jumped, not so much for the thought of that sort of punishment, but for the reality that she'd caused him injury. She'd never meant to do that. "At least..." She avoided his gaze and lowered her voice. "At least until you came along."

No harm, no foul. He stared at her, a few harsh words swirling through his mind. Didn't she know her face was pretty enough to cause grief, all on its own? Didn't she know her lies were dangerous enough to cause heartbreak? Not to him, of course, he was hasty to remind himself. Not at all. But she might have caused a lot of damage. So young to play so casually with people's emotions.

He made a grunting sound of derision. "You didn't harm me, Shannon Harper," he said, and it was mostly true. "But you have made me very angry."

Chapter Five

Marco looked at Shannon, this woman who had made a fool out of him the night before, this person who was nothing but a hired impersonator, this college student with her backpack on the porch, and paradoxically he saw something else. Suddenly she looked impossibly young and just a little scared, and he was overcome with the urge to take her into his arms and hold her.

Wincing, he recoiled, taking a step back away from her. That would be all he needed to complicate his life even further. Better to keep his distance. Besides, he told himself quickly, it was only a natural response. What red-blooded male wouldn't have been provoked by someone this pretty wearing a snug jersey top that emphasized her curves and showed a generous strip of stomach punctuated by a very cute belly button? He was only human. A woman this sexy would make anyone's mouth water. It didn't mean a thing.

"Are you going to let me go?" she was asking, her head cocked to the side in a fashion way too appealing. He could see she was trying to look sassy and sure of herself, but her natural remorse for what she'd done still showed in her eyes. "Or are you planning to prosecute?"

He flashed her a cool look, but he was becoming increasingly aware of how lovely she looked with her hair down around her shoulders. He wasn't supposed to be noticing things like that. "I'm not holding you here," he said rather disingenuously. "You're free to go at any time."

She picked up her purse and started for the door. "So you've finished giving me the third degree," she commented, looking back in a way that made her silky hair swish against her back. "And I survived."

He came up alongside her and reached out to open the door. "I guess you're tougher than you think," he said, looking down at her.

She gave him a dazzling smile as she swirled past him. "Oh, you'd be surprised at how tough I can be, mister," she said as she bounced down the steps. Opening her car door she held out her hand. "My keys?"

Pulling them out of his pocket, he looked at them. Two shiny metal keys were bound together on a key chain with a flat plastic unicorn bearing a large red rose on its chest. He stared at it for a moment, surprised to see the rose, then tossed the set of keys to her. They tumbled through the air, picking up sunlight and shooting out silver sparks. He watched them as though mesmerized, until they landed in her hand and her fingers closed around them. Looking up into her eyes, he saw something change in their violet depths. She stood where she was, looking back at him. He took a step toward her.

"Shannon," he started to say, not sure what he wanted to communicate to her, not sure why he felt this need to keep some kind of contact with her. But he never finished his sentence and whatever it was that had motivated his reaching out for her was lost. Because suddenly, they both became aware that they were not alone.

A TV station film crew van was coming up the driveway. Video cameras were already rolling. A reporter was already shouting questions as he leaned out the window. Two other vans were coming behind them, and he noticed an encampment was being set up across the road from the entrance to the ranch.

"We've got to get out of here," Marco told her, erasing the distance between them in two quick strides. "Come on."

Grabbing her hand and taking the backpack, he rushed her away from her own car and into his low-slung sports number. Swinging into the driver's seat, he gunned the motor and made a direct line toward the vans. There was shouting. Horns honked. People screamed out obscenities. But the vans got out of his way and he roared down the driveway and out onto the road before they could turn around and catch him. In moments they were out of sight of the voracious media.

"Wow." Shannon let out the breath she'd been holding. "Wait a minute." She looked over at him in disbelief. "What just happened here?"

"You've been shanghaied again," he told her calmly. "Learn to live with it."

"But my car…"

"We'll send for it later."

"And my seminar…"

"Call someone for the notes."

She stared at him, breathless. When he decided to take command he didn't mess around. But strangely, it didn't make her angry. Adrenaline was still pumping and she felt closer to laughter than to a retort. And somewhere deep down she knew she was secretly pleased that she was going to be with him for a little longer.

And that, of course, was just plain crazy.

"Where are we going?" she asked him.

"Somewhere safe." He glanced at her. "They've got more pictures now. I'm sure they got a few good ones there as we were leaving." He shook his head impatiently. "They must have had a good response to that picture on the cover of the paper this morning. I can just hear editors now. 'Get out there and find an angle that will give us an excuse to run more on these royals,'" He glanced at her again. "All we need is for someone to track you down and start a story on how you're not the real princess. So I'm afraid you are going to have to go on playing the princess for a little longer."

"What?" Her eyes widened. This was a bit more than she'd counted on. "I thought you considered that perpetrating a fraud."

"I do. But this time you will be working for me."

"Oh. I see." She sank back into the plush seat, enjoying the luxury of all this crushed soft leather and polished wood, along with the jet-speed feeling of skimming just above the ground, but shaking her head. "I guess that makes all the difference."

"Of course it does."

Of course it did.

Surreptitiously, she studied his hands on the dark wood steering wheel. They were strong and yet sculptured, the sort of hands a person could rely on. If nothing else, he was a man who could protect a girl. She had to admit, it made one feel a bit special to be with a man like this. Still, she had to wonder what on earth she was doing here. She should have refused to come along. After all, no good could come of it.

They were heading back into town but he was using an unusual combination of roads to get there, and she had to wonder how he knew so much about Dallas byways.

"I've got a good sense of direction," he told her when she asked.

That made her roll her eyes, but he didn't seem to want to expand on it. He made a couple of calls on his cell phone and she tried hard not to listen in, but she thought she caught the gist of what was said. Still, she was surprised when he pulled into the underground parking lot of a hotel on the other side of town.

"I thought you were staying at the same hotel where the ball was held last night," she said.

"I was. But we always book a backup hotel under a different name just in case."

She frowned at him. "In case of what?"

He pulled carefully into a parking spot and turned off the engine, turning in his seat to face her. It was dark in the underground parking area and his face was shadowed, but his teeth gleamed white as he talked.

"My family has always been obsessed with staying out of the media spotlight. We don't want to end up like so many royals do, as fodder for the tabloids. When there's a problem, we tend to disappear from sight."

"So you're trying to hide from those people out at the ranch?"

He winced. "*Hide* isn't the word I would use," he objected. "*Avoid* is better. We're avoiding anyone who might think they have us in their sights."

He paused for a moment, looking at her and she searched the depths of his ice-blue eyes, wondering if she would be able to find any hint of interest there, any sense that he saw her as a woman instead of an inconvenience. But there was nothing. Did he feel nothing at all? Or was he just that good at hiding it?

He opened his door and began to rise from his seat, grabbing her backpack as he did so.

She hopped out to join him, then came to a screeching halt. "Wait a minute," she said as realization dawned. "I can't go up to your room with you."

He stopped and looked back at her, frowning. "Why not?"

She opened her mouth, then closed it again. "It just isn't done, that's all."

"Oh. That." His face cleared. "Don't worry. My man, Jordan will chaperone. He's already here, preparing the suite for us."

She hesitated and he got impatient. "Oh come on, Shannon," he said. "My intentions are entirely honorable, I promise you that. We just need to keep you under wraps until this blows over. If anyone from the press gets to you and begins to ferret out your real identity, the story will be nationwide, believe me.''

She frowned. She knew there were holes in this theory but she couldn't put her finger on them right away. And he seemed so sure of himself. Thinking quickly, she decided to play along for the time being, but to keep her guard up, just in case.

''All right,'' she said at last. ''But no Bluebeard's Castle stuff.''

The look that came over his face surprised her, but his control reasserted itself quickly. ''Don't worry,'' he said calmly. ''Jordan doesn't allow it.''

''Good.''

She'd only been half joking. Not that she really suspected him of anything underhanded, but after all, she'd certainly done enough to him to make payback a consideration. But she knew he wasn't the vindictive type. Revenge would be beneath him. Risking a covert glance his way, she felt a little frisson of excitement as she contemplated spending more time with him. Crown prince or not, he was a man made to arouse female interest.

They took the gleaming elevator to the twelfth floor and walked into a suite of rooms that took Shannon's breath away—glass tables, brass accessories, leather upholstery, carpets so thick she was afraid she would get lost in the plush fibers if she fell, and huge arrangements of flowers everywhere. She was still staring around with her mouth open when she realized someone else had entered the room.

She'd seen Marco's valet before, but this was the first time she'd paid much attention. Tall and stately with a long, mournful face, he looked exactly like what she thought he should look like. He didn't change expression at the sight of her, though she knew his all-seeing gaze had taken in her bare midriff and snug jeans and did not approve.

"Jordan, this is Miss Shannon Harper."

"I am pleased to make your acquaintance, Miss Harper," he said with a slight bow and a tone that didn't show any pleasure at all.

A part of her wanted to draw back like a scalded puppy. She knew she looked like something the cat dragged in compared to what he was used to seeing in the women Marco knew. But there was another part of her that got its dander up from what she perceived just might be his attitude. She was an American, darn it all, and she was going to act like one.

So instead of cringing, she stepped forward and stuck her hand out, forcing him to shake it, and said, "I'm very pleased to meet *you*, Mr. Jordan. I assume you are the arbiter of all things in manners and morals that go on around here. Since I'm just a novice at this royalty stuff, I'll be happy to take advice on any issue you deem pertinent."

Forced to shake hands against his wont, Jordan looked stricken and performed the deed as though taking hold of a dead fish. Very quickly, he mumbled something and turned to go. Marco could hardly contain his soft laughter until the man was out of the room.

"I have never seen such a look on Jordan's face before," he whispered to her, still chuckling. "Shannon Harper...." He shook his head.

He wanted to say something about her. Something

nice. She could tell by the provocative gleam in his eye. And she wanted more than anything to hear him say it. Her gaze slid to his mouth and she wondered what his kiss would be like. With him looking at her like this, there was hope along those lines as well.

But not for long. Within seconds, that sexy gleam faded and he sobered and turned away. She sighed, hugging her arms to her shoulders.

Why was it that every time he seemed to be on the verge of making a connection with her, just a simple human reaching out and acknowledging, he backed away?

Still, it was probably just as well. There were two elements here that she knew of. First, he was going to be marrying Iliana whether he wanted to or not. And second, there was his abiding love for his wife. She knew Lorraine haunted him. She could see it in his eyes. This was a man no woman was ever going to get close to again.

Jordan returned. He'd obviously managed to recover quickly, because he was looking as though nothing had happened, and when Marco said, ''Jordan, please show Miss Harper to her room,'' he bowed and turned to do exactly that.

''My room?'' Shannon swung around to stare at the prince. ''You mean I'm staying overnight?''

''I thought you understood, Shannon. You'll be staying here until we find Princess Iliana and get her back here to take up the role.''

She stared at him suspiciously, her hands on her hips. ''Now you wait just a darn minute here.''

Marco looked weary, just about at the end of his rope. ''Shannon, go to your room,'' he said.

Luckily there was just enough of a request in his tone, rather than a command, that she felt she could comply without losing her dignity. So she took a deep breath and did as he asked, following Jordan into a huge bedroom—which she immediately fell in love with. Floor-to-ceiling windows were framed by beautiful drapes held back with heavy gold cord, and the bed had a canopy.

"Oh!" she said, turning slowly to look at it all. A bedroom a princess could love.

"You will note there is a telephone beside the bed," Jordan told her. "May I request that, should you make a call, you not reveal your current location. And please keep such calls short, so they can't be traced."

She gave him a wide-eyed look and nodded.

"There is a television, a DVD player, a stack of magazines," he continued. "If you think of anything else you need to make your stay comfortable, please let me know."

"Oh, I will."

"I took the liberty of having a few frocks sent up for you." He opened the sliding door to the walk-in closet so that she could peruse them.

"'Frocks?'"she said, wrinkling her nose. But then she saw them. Blue silk, pink organdy, and some green clinging material, shimmery dresses and sleek pantsuits. "Oh my," she said faintly. These things were as nice or nicer than anything Greta had picked from Iliana's inventory for her to wear as the princess over the last few weeks.

"Feel free to investigate at will," Jordan said in

his usual snooty tone, but she thought she saw a spark of fear in his eyes as she turned and grinned at him.

"I'll do that. And thank you for all you've done for me so far," she told him.

She waited, hoping he would say, "Your wish is my command," like some human genie, but he merely nodded, bowed, and left the room quickly, as though he were afraid she might give him a hug if he didn't move fast enough.

Shrugging, she looked at the huge bed, made a jumping start and dove onto it, rolling in the soft luxury of it all. This was the life! Rising, she wandered around for a few minutes, spent some time looking down at the people in the street, looking like ants at this height, and finally flopped down on the bed again, picked up the remote and turned on the television.

Flipping from one channel to another, she came upon a movie that looked interesting. Audrey Hepburn in *Roman Holiday*. Watching, she began to realize the story was about a romance between a princess and a commoner. Now her attention was engaged and she was riveted to the screen, though she felt a little guilty. Her mother would not have approved. When she was young her mother wouldn't let her watch anything with a compelling love story—especially any such thing with royalty involved.

"I don't want your mind filled with that sort of claptrap," she would say. "Girls who let love blind them to reality always come to a bad end. You're going to learn to stand on your own two feet. You don't need a man to make you happy."

There was some justification for her mother's feelings. She'd had a hard life. As a single mom, she'd often had to work two jobs to keep Shannon and herself provided for. And her rather short marriage to Grant Harper had ended unhappily. So Shannon could see a reason for her mother's attitude.

Still, it was hard for her to keep dreams out of her head and her heart. She watched the touching story on the television screen until the final poignant scene.

She sniffed and realized tears had welled, distorting her vision. Sighing, she blotted her eyes with a tissue and lay back against the pillows, thinking of life and love and the vagaries of fate. And royalty.

But that didn't last long. She'd had enough of this lying around. Rolling off the bed, she practiced putting her hair up, trying to look like Audrey Hepburn, and decided against it. She just didn't have the elfin quality necessary for the look. But she was getting restless here in the room and she figured it was about time to venture forth and see what was going on in the rest of the world. She did change into one of the soft, flowing pantsuits and then she opened the door and peeked out.

Marco was sitting at a desk, working on some papers, frowning. He definitely looked as though he needed rescuing from that boring task. What he could use was a little bit of distracting. She could do that.

"Hi," she said breezily, venturing forth. "Mind if I come out and hang with you for a while?"

Putting his pen down, he turned and looked at her, and his expression was almost benign. That was a first.

"Fine," he said. "It's time for tea anyway. Would you like some?"

"Tea? As in afternoon tea, with scones and little cakes and things?"

He nodded.

She brightened considerably, sitting down to join him around the low glass coffee table. "That would be wonderful."

Jordan materialized with a tray without even having to be asked. Shannon leaned forward, studying the beautiful little creations being presented for her nourishment. Afternoon tea—it sounded like something Audrey Hepburn would have.

"They're too beautiful to eat," she announced as she popped one little sandwich into her mouth. "But they taste too good to pass up," she added. "So I feel like I'm desecrating little masterpieces."

"Thank you, Jordan," Marco said as his valet poured tea for them both. He eyed Shannon eating with gusto and making appreciative noises. "Better make sure there's a second round just in case."

Jordan bowed and left them. Shannon looked up at Marco from under her long lashes. "I know I'm embarrassing you, but these are just so good!"

"You're not embarrassing me," he told her, leaning back in his chair to watch her with something that might almost have been a smile hovering on his lips. "I don't get embarrassed by much."

She took a round chocolate cup filled with custard and savored it before responding. "This is very nice. You have quite a life, you royals." Then she frowned, remembering some of the things she'd learned about them and their sort lately. "But I guess being royal isn't all fun and games, is it?"

"Not by a long shot."

He said it in a world-weary way that made her stop and look at him more closely. Something was worrying him. Was it this Princess Iliana business? And hiding out from the media? Or was there more to it?

"Are you glad?" she asked him softly, waiting to see if she could read his answer in his eyes.

"About what?"

She shrugged. "To be taking over. To be king."

Nothing changed. Or maybe it did, because his gaze was suddenly a darker blue than usual. But she couldn't tell what that meant.

"I have no choice," he said quietly. "It's my responsibility."

He was always so serious. She wished she knew a way to lighten his spirits without making him angry—because anything that only ended up doing that wasn't going to work at all.

"Yes," she said, "but do you accept that responsibility joyfully or with bitter resignation?"

"Neither." He looked fully into her eyes. "I'd say I accept it with a quiet satisfaction as long as I am able to do the job right."

She shook her head. Her heart had jumped when their gazes had connected, but she didn't want him to know that. She was reacting to him more and more. If she didn't know better, she would almost think she was coming down with a very healthy crush on the man. "I wouldn't be able to stand it."

"Why? It's just a job. Everybody has to have a job."

"It's also a way of life."

He looked past her, considering for a moment. "That's true."

"And even if you are successful in keeping the media away from your family for the most part, there is so much pressure. You're basically living for other people all the time."

He looked pained. "To some extent. But I am well compensated, you know. There are a few perks that come with the job."

"Sure." She threw out her hand as though she hardly counted all that. "Money. Travel. Castles to live in."

He smiled, then quickly erased it. "I was thinking more along the lines of power."

"Power." She wrinkled her nose.

"Yes, Shannon. Power."

This was a concept she had never really thought about. "Do you enjoy power?" she asked, just a bit skeptical.

"Yes. I do. With the right sort of power, you can change things. But I also feel a very strong responsibility to wield it in a way that will make the lives of the people of my country better. If in the end I haven't done that I will have failed as a monarch."

She sat back, her cup of tea in her hands, and studied him. He seemed to mean what he was saying and she admired that. If he really did care the way he said he did, she was going to have to revise some of the prejudices she'd had drilled into her since childhood about kings and princes and the careless way they dealt with people's lives.

"I was actually raised with a great deal of scorn for royalty," she told him confidentially.

"Why?" He looked outraged. "You're an American. Why would the topic even come up?"

"My mother was Nabotavian."

"Ah." One dark eyebrow rose. "That's a surprise."

She nodded. "It never seemed odd to me. It was just a part of who I was, who my mother was. But since I've met all you Alovitians and Nabotavians, I've realized my upbringing was pretty unique."

"I'd say so. Did you know any other Nabotavians when you were young?"

"No. Only my mother's close friend, Jay. She often came to visit us. But other than that, I looked at Nabotavia as a sort of fairy-tale land, not completely real, but still, a part of me." She smiled, remembering. "Funny, huh?"

"So why was your mother against the royalty?" he asked her.

She looked at him sideways, realizing any royalty her mother had hated must have been a part of his extended family. "I don't know exactly what happened to her when she was young," she said, half teasing now, "but she always told me, 'Shannon, stay away from crown princes.'"

"Did she?" The corners of his mouth quirked.

"Oh yes." She gave him a wise look. "She was convinced they were up to no good."

"And she was probably right," he said smoothly. "But there are exceptions to every rule."

"Don't tell me. Let me guess." She pointed a finger at him. "You're that very exception. Am I right?"

He nodded slowly, holding her gaze. "You know you are," he said.

Her heart jumped, then began to beat much faster. Did he know how sexy he looked, gazing at her that way? Probably not. Because she was sure he didn't mean to provoke her in a sensual way. That would be so out of bounds.... She shivered. She didn't even want to think about it.

Jordan came in to take away the tea things and she took the opportunity to change the subject.

"What time is it?" she said, moving nervously in her seat.

Marco shot back his cuff and looked at his gold watch. "It's almost five. Perhaps you need to call someone to let them know where you are?"

She thought for a moment. "Not really," she said.

There weren't many people who would miss her. That seemed sort of sad now that she thought about it. How had she managed to work her life into this? Over the last few years she'd been totally concentrated on taking care of her mother during her grave illness, and then she'd thrown herself heart and soul into her studies at the university.

"I suppose I really should call Randy at the steakhouse and see if I've still got a job."

He raised an eyebrow and looked at his valet. "Jordan will take care of that," he said, raising an eyebrow at his man, who nodded. "What else."

"Well..."

"You don't have a date with that cowboy?"

"What cowboy?" She frowned at him. "You don't mean Jody? Oh, he's just an old friend."

Jordan switched on a lamp and Marco's gaze seemed to sparkle in the new light.

"Surely you have a young man in your life," he said, his calm voice belied by some sort of undercurrent she couldn't really identify.

"No. Sorry to disappoint you, but I'm not the domestic type." She tossed back her hair. "I have no interest in settling down and being a doormat for some man. So I don't bother to date."

He looked as though he thought she was joking again. "You expect me to believe that?"

"I'm quite serious. I'm aiming for a career, probably in museum curating. I don't have time for romantic games."

She could tell him about how her mother had drilled into her how she should never trust a man. But then he would think her mother had been some sort of nutcase, and that wasn't really true. Her mother had had a pretty rough life and she'd tried to give her daughter the benefit of her own mistakes. Shannon didn't know who her biological father was, and the man who adopted her and gave her his name ran off with a younger woman by the time Shannon was eleven. That, along with some of her own experiences, had taught her that her mother was right.

Romance was all very well and good, but she would never, ever let herself get carried away. You could depend on an education, a job, a career, but you couldn't depend on a man. Too many girls forgot about that.

He was staring at her in a strange way and she thought he was on the verge of saying something, but he stopped himself before he got it out and gave her a dismissive nod.

"All right," he said shortly. "You'd better go back to your room and let me get some work done. Dinner will be at seven, right here in the suite. I'll see you then."

She frowned, resenting his tone and the abrupt dismissal. But after all, she was nothing but an encumbrance to him, so what did she expect? Rising, she turned to go, but looked back at him just before disappearing into the bedroom. He was bent over his paperwork again, but his face didn't look as weary as it had. Good. Maybe she was of some benefit to him after all.

Chapter Six

Marco threw down his pen. There was no use pretending. Shannon was ruining his concentration. Even when she wasn't in the room he could smell the scent she wore. It reminded him of sunrise and butterflies and a fresh breeze off the meadow. He kept thinking about the way her hair curled around her ear, and the way her hands fluttered like birds when she talked, and the way her laugh seemed to play on his heart strings like a harpist with magic in her fingers. Even now he could see her long, lean legs under that filmy fabric someone had nonsensically concocted into a pair of pants, and beads of sweat seemed to form on his upper lip as he thought of them.

It was all too crazy, of course. There was no doubt that she was attractive. There was no doubt that he wanted her. But it was just a biological thing. He couldn't have been less interested, actually. After all, he loved his wife and he was going to marry Princess

Iliana. If he was going to start falling for anyone, it had to be her. Lorraine…well, Lorraine would understand that he had to move on. It had been two years, two long and very lonely years. He needed someone. The way he was going silly over this girl proved that. It was time he settled down—before he made a fool of himself over someone like Shannon.

But he knew he shouldn't have barked at her the way he'd done a half hour before when she'd come out and tried to strike up a conversation. He'd told her to wait until she was called for dinner, and he'd seen the hurt outrage in her eyes. She felt he'd insulted her. It was better that she didn't know that he'd taken one look at her pretty, sleepy face and felt desire rise in him so hard and strong that he'd been angry at himself as much as anything when he'd reacted that way. He couldn't let this go on. She was just too…adorable.

She was coming out now and he was going to give her a simple smile of welcome. That ought to show her he meant her no disrespect. Jordan had laid out the table very nicely, with red roses as a centerpiece and bone china at each place. The entrée was poached salmon with asparagus and a rice pilaf. A crisp Caesar salad was served in its own bowl, and a very dry Chardonnay filled the wine goblets. Heavy sterling silver flatware put the final touch on an elegant meal.

He looked at her expectantly as she strolled toward the table, but she didn't meet his gaze. Instead, she stood a few feet away and looked at the beautiful setting.

''Where's Jordan?'' she asked.

"Jordan?" He frowned, puzzled. "I don't know. In the other room I suppose."

Her chin rose and she stared at the far wall. "Shouldn't I be eating with him?"

He stared at her. "What are you talking about?"

"Well, he's hired help and so am I. Don't you think I belong with him instead of in here with the grand crown prince?"

Obviously, she was still upset. He grimaced. "Don't be ridiculous," he said shortly. "You're here because I want you here."

"Oh. I suppose that settles that." She threw him a glare. "It's all about what you want, is it?"

He resisted the temptation to respond in kind. Instead, he pulled out her chair for her and made a gesture of invitation. She hesitated long enough to let him know she hated him—for the moment—and then sat in the chair, letting him push it in for her.

She put her napkin in her lap but avoided his gaze, and her own had a smoky, rebellious look to it. Her mouth was almost pouting. She looked incredibly appealing and he was beginning to think an ice-cold shower was going to be his only hope for salvation.

With a sudden flash of insight, he knew that she was waiting for an apology from him, just as she had on the dance floor the night before. Well, that was too bad, because she damn well wasn't going to get one.

"Eat your vegetables," he said gruffly.

"*You* eat them," she responded.

"Me? I've already eaten mine. Why would I eat yours?"

"Because everything belongs to you, doesn't it? You're the crown prince."

That statement was so ludicrous, he gaped at her. Her gaze met his and they stared at each other for a long moment, and then, reluctantly, he grinned, and she pressed her lips together, trying to stop the laughter that was bubbling up her throat. But she couldn't and then they were both laughing.

He stuck out his hand. "Friends?" he asked her.

She looked at it for a moment, then stuck out her own and took his in it. "Friends," she agreed.

"Good." He went back to eating. "Now maybe we can both enjoy this delicious dinner."

"Hmm," she agreed.

Taking a bite of her salad, she contemplated the man. It had been a little silly to take such offense at his impatience with her earlier, but it had helped to keep a distance between them for a few minutes. And it was important that the distance be maintained. There was a natural attraction between the two of them. She didn't think he could deny it any more than she could. So it was just as well he was going to be marrying someone else. Just as well.

Not that she herself didn't have a hankering to get a little closer. Despite all the best efforts of her own mother, here she was, mooning over a man—and a royal no less.

"Mama," she whispered silently, biting her lip. "I'm sorry. But he is so very handsome."

A sudden epiphany flashed in from the more sensible side of her character—the left side of her brain—and ruined the easy fantasy of the right side. If she thought all there was here was an attraction to a gorgeous man, she was sadly deluded. "Natural attraction, my foot!" the left side sneered. "You're in danger of falling for the man, honey."

She stared straight ahead and tried to push the discordant voice back down where she'd been keeping it. She couldn't afford to fall for him. There was no future in it. So she wasn't going to do it. End of issue.

Jordan served them light cups of mint ice cream for dessert, and they ate slowly, talking about great meals they'd had, books they'd read and classes they'd taken. Soon the ice cream was melting in the bowls as they became involved in a heated discussion about whether surfing belonged in Olympic competition, and when Jordan finally came back to clear the table, they were shocked to realize how late it was.

Retiring to the couches, they went on talking, hardly noticing Jordan as he hovered in the background tidying up the room and putting on some music to provide a background. And that only brought up a new topic as they argued about whether Gershwin should be considered a musical great along with the European masters.

Marco enjoyed the passion she displayed as she made her case, and suddenly he realized how unusual she was. How many women of his acquaintance cared about such things? When he finally asked her where she got her interest, she laughed.

"My mother was once a child prodigy on the piano," she told him. "She made sure I had a well-rounded education in classical music, literature, art, the whole gamut. I'll always be grateful to her for that." She looked a little sad for a moment, then her warm smile came back and she brought up the subject of her art history obsession.

"I'm doing my dissertation on Havel Dirksonian," she told him. "And that's one reason why I was interested in taking the job of pretending to be a princess from that part of the world."

Marco frowned thoughtfully. "Why does that name sound vaguely familiar?"

"Vaguely familiar!" She gaped at him, truly affronted. "He's only the best Nabotavian artist of the twentieth century. I can't believe you don't know who he is."

Grabbing her backpack, which she'd brought out of the bedroom, she pulled out one of her textbooks. "Here. Come and look at some of his work." She opened the book on the glass coffee table and he came over and sat beside her so that he could see it better.

Havel Dirksonian worked on large canvasses, using color as much to display emotion as form. She pointed out pictures of a couple of her favorites, and Marco frowned at them, looking first from one angle, then from another.

"Okay," he said, looking up into her eager face. "I guess it's the sort of thing that grows on you, isn't it?"

"What?" She couldn't believe he could be so thick about art. "These paintings are magnificent. Don't you see it?"

He looked again, hoping to see what she was obviously so excited about. But no. Big splashes of color. That was about it. "Not really," he admitted at last.

"Oh!" She threw her hands up in the air. "I can't

believe this." Frowning down at the pictures in the book, she shook her head. "Really, these pictures don't give you any idea of the grandeur and scope of his paintings." She looked up at him. "You have to go to the Stygina Museum in the Arts district. They have a number of Dirksonians on exhibit right now." Her face lit up with an idea. "You want to go?"

"Go?"

"To the museum. Tomorrow." She tugged on his arm, her eyes sparkling. "Oh come on. You're going to be blown away. I promise."

Her enthusiasm made him smile, and it seemed to be contagious. At least a little. "We'd have to go in disguises," he noted, but his words let her know he was weakening and she laughed aloud.

"Great. I'm used to that."

He met her gaze and something seemed to snap and crackle between them. Her smile began to fade and she withdrew her hand from his arm, suddenly looking confused.

"Wow, look at the time," she said, and it was almost midnight. "I guess I'd better get some sleep." She rose, looking about the room, then back at him. "Don't forget. We're going to the museum in the morning," she said. Throwing him a saucy smile and giving his valet a friendly wave, she headed for her bedroom. "Good night," she called back, and then her door closed.

Marco sat very still, decompressing from her presence. He had to admit he liked her. She was certainly fun to have around. In fact, he was already sure that he was going to miss her when this was over and she wasn't around any longer. But that was just the way life was. Unpredictable. And usually relatively unpleasant.

"So, it's disguises for tomorrow, Jordan," he said to his valet.

"Sir?" Jordan looked down his long nose disapprovingly.

Marco grinned. "Don't give me that look, Jordan. Miss Harper is going to take me out and introduce me to the finer elements of Nabotavian art."

The valet looked startled. "Sir?"

Marco laughed as he rose to go back to his desk and finish his paperwork. "You just deal with finding Iliana. I'll figure out how to deal with Miss Harper."

Jordan's long face looked even more mournful than usual. "I certainly hope so, sir."

There was a rustle of wind in the high treetops above him and something brushed his cheek. A woman laughed.

"Lorraine," he thought, turning to try to catch sight of her as she disappeared behind the greenery. But it wasn't Lorraine. It was something else, a white bird with a long, drooping tail that floated past him and then turned as he reached for it and flew to a high branch, too high for his grasp....

He woke with a start. He'd fallen asleep on his work and he was stiff and a little cold. But there was something....

"I'm sorry," Shannon said softly. "I didn't mean to wake you."

He blinked, his mind foggy, not sure if he was still dreaming for a moment. She looked like a spirit with her long nightgown covered with an even longer robe.

The material seemed to float around her, and so did her hair. For a moment he was tempted to reach out and see if his hand would go right through her.

But half a second later he was glad he hadn't tried it.

"Why are you still working?" she was asking. "It's almost two in the morning."

He nodded, yawning. She was right. "I'm going to bed," he agreed. Then he frowned. "What are you doing up?"

She shrugged. "I don't know. I was reading a book, and then I thought I would catch *Roman Holiday* again. It just ended. And I cried again."

His frown deepened. She seemed so happy about the crying thing. Women were strange. "Why did you cry?"

"Because the princess gave up the man she loved for her people." She sniffed happily. "Sort of like you," she said.

He thought for a moment. Maybe he was still too full of sleep to make connections but for the life of him he couldn't make any sense out of what she'd said and he decided to ignore it. But one thing he couldn't ignore was how very appealing she looked, soft and sleepy, her mouth rubbed free of makeup but all the more kissable because of it. He wanted to take her in his arms, more out of a feeling of affection than desire. But even affection could lead to danger and he knew enough to hold off the impulse.

"Tell you what," he said instead, rising and stretching a bit. "Let's go into the kitchen and grab a snack, then we'll both go and get some sleep."

"Okay," she said agreeably. "Which way is it?"

He led her into Jordan's domain. Everything was gleaming and spotless. Opening the little refrigerator, he pulled out a few leftover tarts from their afternoon tea.

"Will this do?" he asked her.

She nodded happily. "Those were so good."

Pulling out two plates, he set up a couple of tarts on each and set them on the table. She marveled at him even as she sat down to eat her share.

"I didn't know crown princes could be so handy in the kitchen," she said. "Do you do omelets?"

"My specialty," he said, and he almost offered to make her one in the morning, but he bit his tongue and held off just in time. There were too many connotations of a love affair involved with that scenario. Best to let it go.

They ate in silence for a few minutes. Shannon hardly noticed what she was putting in her mouth. Her thoughts were full of Marco. She'd never known a man like him before.

He was so serious, and yet every now and then his sense of humor poked through and showed itself. He was so carefully controlled, and yet he responded to her on a man-woman level. The evidence revealed itself for whole seconds at a time. Some might think she was dreaming, but she knew better. He liked what he saw when he looked at her. And she liked having him look. If only he weren't a prince and they could let that feeling grow.

But he was a prince, and he was going to marry a princess. Give it up, Shannon, she told herself. Don't go making silly moves you'll only live to regret. Remember the warnings!

But it was hard to remember those wobbly little scaredy-cat warnings when the man was so close and his eyes were blue as a summer sky and his delicious scent was so male. Even so, in a moment he would rise from the table and say good-night. Suddenly she wanted more than anything to keep him here a little longer.

What could she ask him? What could she get him to talk about that would keep him near her for another half hour? Ah yes! She'd forgotten her resolution to get as much out of this exposure to the Nabotavian royalty as she could. Maybe he could give her some new insights, or at least an anecdote or two.

"I really don't know much about your immediate family," she told him. "There's not much in the literature or the media about the Roseanovas."

He nodded. "That's the way we like it. And want to keep it."

"So I've noticed." She gave him her most winsome smile. "Still, you might give me just a little glimpse of what your family is like."

"A glimpse." His mouth twisted into a half smile and his gaze flickered over her, then withdrew as though she cast too bright a light. "That's all the tabloid writers ask for as well. Just a glimpse."

She gasped and he added quickly, "No I'm not accusing you of being a spy. I'm just so used to being careful, suspicions are part of my everyday attitude now." He glanced into her eyes to see if she understood, then frowned when he saw he'd hurt her again. Unfortunately, no matter how he tried to avoid it, that was going to keep happening. He mulled over what he could tell her that might make up for it. He was sure she already knew the background, how his family belonged to the House of the Red Rose, the Roseanovas, who ruled Nabotavia for hundreds of years, how twenty years ago a coalition of opposition groups got together and staged a coup, taking over the country and killing his parents, King Marcovo and Queen Marie. So he began his story with the escape, telling her about how he and his brothers and sister were smuggled out of the country and made their to the USA.

"My brother Garth and sister Karina were hidden in a secret place behind the bench of an old wagon," he told her. "I was older, about twelve, so I was too big to hide that way. They dressed me as a schoolboy with a little cap on my head and gave me a bicycle to ride. I had to stay as far as possible from the rest of them so that they wouldn't know we were together. The guards questioned me at the border. I remember I was so nervous riding toward them that my front wheel wobbled badly, so one of the guards made me get off and took a look at my tire for me." He smiled, remembering.

"That must have made you even more nervous," she said, studying his handsome face.

"The funny thing was it did just the opposite. A strange calm came over me and suddenly I knew it was going to be okay. I felt a power inside...." He shrugged, not attempting to explain it. "I sometimes get that way when I'm very sure of what I'm doing," he said softly, more to himself than to her.

But she nodded. She'd seen that confidence in him. She couldn't help but admire it.

"Anyway, the younger generation all made it out

okay and we've all been raised here and we love this country. But we belong to Nabotavia and we have worked from the beginning to free our land. Now that we've won her freedom, we are going back.''

She sighed. It was a touching story, part tragedy, part adventure. She couldn't help but see Marco as the hero, leading the others. That was what he was born for, of course, but it was more than that. She knew he'd be the hero of her dreams even if he weren't headed for the throne. "And since you are next in succession, in January you will be crowned. You'll be King Marco.''

He nodded. "Yes, that's right.''

She looked at him and once again, her admiration blossomed. He had the weight of his country, of all his people's hopes and fears, their very destiny, on his shoulders. And he accepted that responsibility with grace and determination. He was ready to do what had to be done, to go and be their king, make the decisions that would guide their futures. If he guessed wrong, if he made a bad decision, their anguish would be his fault. It was an awesome burden. It took a pair of strong, broad shoulders, and he had them.

But she had to wonder if he might not have a little too much hubris, a little too much easy assurance that he would do well by his country. Did he also have the humility necessary to become a great leader? That was probably still up in the air.

"Tell me about your brothers and sister," she coaxed.

"I have only one sister." He smiled as he thought of her. "She's the baby of the family."

"Karina," Shannon said.

"Yes. She just married a young man named Jack Santini. So now, I guess, her name is Karina Santini-Roseanova."

Shannon smiled. She already knew the names of his siblings but she enjoyed hearing him talk about hem. "And your brothers?"

"I'm the oldest, of course. And next comes Garth. He's considered the warrior of the family. Recently he agreed to marry a princess from the White Rose Roseanovas, a branch of the royal family, who he'd been betrothed to for years. He'd been resisting. I wasn't sure we would ever see him settle down, but it seems he's fallen in love with her, much as he tried to resist, and he's decided he can do it after all."

"Love leads the way?" she asked blithely.

"Either that, or love is blind," he quoted with a cynicism that would have done her mother proud.

She made a face. "But he did fall in love, didn't he? That's wonderful."

His nod was almost grudging. "Then there is the youngest boy, Damian. He's engaged as well, to a woman named Sara Joplin. He's always been the playboy, so we are all very pleased that he is going to marry a good, levelheaded woman."

"Is she royal?"

"Not at all. She's an American. Actually, he had an accident that rendered him temporarily blind and she was his therapist."

She tried to picture a room full of Roseanova men. "And you're all going back in January?"

"Yes. We're all going back."

"And all the brothers are getting married at the same time?"

He hesitated. "Well, I don't think there are any plans for a triple wedding," he began, then frowned and stopped right where he was. The thought was appalling.

But Shannon didn't seem to think so. She sighed at the romance of it all. "All the others are marrying people that they love, aren't they?" she noted, flashing him a quick look.

His expression darkened. "I already married the woman that I love," he said gruffly.

She nodded slowly, wondering if he had any idea how that statement cut into her like the thrust of a dagger. It shouldn't, but it did. She knew, suddenly, that she would never know another man like this. That brought a lump to her throat and she had to wait while it slowly faded.

"Look," she said at last. "I know it's none of my business. I know I'm just a hired imposter who is more of a burden to you than anything else."

He started to speak but she shook her head and put up her hand to stop him. "I just want to tell you something. I've been close to the situation now, and I've seen how the land lies. I've seen things about Princess Iliana. I've pretended to be her, for heaven's sake, and as such, I've put myself in her place in many ways." She frowned, trying hard to look as earnest as she felt. "I've seen you and how you react and what kind of a man you are."

Her voice broke a little on the word *man* and something changed in his eyes and she went on quickly, before he could stop her. "Okay, you may hate me for this. You may never speak to me again. You may banish me to the far end of the moon for all I know.''

He tried to smile but the effect was almost painful to see. ''Shannon, even as King of Nabotavia, I don't think I will quite have the power to do that.''

She took a full breath, as though getting ready to dive into the deep end. ''Maybe not. But you may want to.'' Reaching out, she grabbed hold of his hand. He felt warm to her cool fingers. She would have loved to bring his warmth to her lips, but that would probably be taking things a little too far.

''I have to say something. I know you loved Lorraine in a wonderful, uplifting way that still lasts in you. Most any woman would give her soul to be loved like that.''

He looked into her eyes and knew he didn't want to hear what she was going to say next. ''Shannon,'' he began sternly, but she ignored him.

''But don't you see? That is exactly why it would be a crime if you married Iliana.''

''Shannon…''

''Wait.'' She squeezed his hand tightly. ''Listen. You don't love her. Once she comes back, if you find it possible to fall in love with her, well…then whatever I say here will be moot. But I don't think it's going to happen that way.'' She held his hand in hers as though she were holding on to a lifeline. ''Please don't marry her just because you promised her father you would. And please don't marry her just because you feel you need to be married.''

He shook his head. ''Shannon, you don't know what you're talking about,'' he said harshly.

''I know that. But….'' Suddenly her eyes were

swimming with tears. "The love you had with Lorraine was a beautiful thing. I know that you think, because you've already had that, it can't come again and so it won't matter who you marry. But it will, Marco. It will matter a great deal." Her voice broke but she went on huskily. "If you marry Iliana for the wrong reasons, it will make you hard and cynical and bitter and the love you have for Lorraine will be sullied by that. I don't know how I know this, but I do."

He sat very still, saying nothing, but staring hard into the depths of her eyes. Tears were pooling in them, but that only made them sparkle more brightly.

"Okay," she said, withdrawing her hand and feeling a little foolish. "Now you can hate me. I'm going to bed." She rose and looked down at him. "But Marco, I…I think a lot of you. And what I've said I only expressed out of my regard for you. Please think it over." She touched his cheek with the back of her hand, he started to lift his hand, whether to push hers away, or to cover it, she didn't know, because he never completed the gesture, letting it drop back onto the table. She swallowed hard and turned, then hurried to her room.

He closed his eyes, surprised that they were stinging. He heard her leave the room but he didn't look up. With his eyes closed, everything was black. That felt right, somehow. Some nights were too dark for tears.

Chapter Seven

"Cowboy boots? You want me to wear cowboy boots?" Marco gazed at her in astonishment.

"You're darn right I do. You wanted a disguise. Well, honey," Shannon said, going into a thick Texas drawl, "dressing like a Texan is about as far from being a Nabotavian crown prince as you can get." She grinned. "And anyway, you look darn manly in 'em."

He grumbled, but she could see the spark of humor in his eyes. He seemed a little wobbly in the boots at first, but he soon got the hang of wearing them. The jeans went over much more easily, as well as the plaid shirt. But the Stetson drew another look of skepticism from him.

"I don't wear hats," he told her, holding it at arm's length.

"Texans wear these," she responded sunnily. "If you're going to dress like a Texan…"

He put on the hat. She stood back nodding her approval. She'd never seen a cowboy looking better. "You were born for this," she told him, and he actually laughed aloud. But she noticed he picked up on the Texas swagger right away, walking with the masculine stride that bespoke working ponies in the hot sun on the long-ago trail. Watching him gave her a little quiver of appreciation. He sure was an appealing man.

The night before she'd been afraid that telling him what she really thought would destroy any relationship between them forever. She'd been sure that this morning there would be a new coolness and a distancing—that he might even have left before she got up to avoid having to face her and she might never see him again. She'd emerged from her room with her heart in her throat, sure that he would be gone.

But no. She'd found him reading the morning paper and when she'd tentatively said, "Good morning," he'd looked up and smiled at her. The smile had taken her breath away. There had been something new in it, something that reached out and touched her. She almost felt as though she'd been kissed. But just as quickly the sense of connection was gone. Then he'd invited her into the kitchen where he pushed Jordan out of the way and cooked her a most delicious omelet for her breakfast. They'd talked, sporadically at first, then more and more naturally, until they were laughing together almost like old friends.

And now she was dressing him up as a Texan.

"What's your disguise going to be?" he asked her.

"I could just go as Shannon Harper," she said. "But that wouldn't be any fun. So I think I'll try

Audrey Hepburn.'' She didn't have any Givenchy suits on hand, but she wore a beautifully tailored marled jersey knit top she found in the closet, along with slim ribbed-knit slacks and suede flats. Jamming huge sunglasses on her nose, she pulled a long scarf tightly around her head and turned to look at him questioningly. ''What do you think?''

''Not bad,'' he said, and his admiration for her shone in his brilliant eyes in a way that couldn't be concealed.

She swallowed hard, feeling a little breathless. He was definitely coming out of his defensive shell. Was she sure she knew how to handle a crown prince unleashed? Talk about playing with fire.

Jordan hovered in the background looking disapproving, but she was getting used to that and Marco didn't seem to notice. Once they were ready, dressed in their new clothes that were supposed to help them blend into the Dallas scene, he ordered up a rental car, a small sedan that no self-respecting crown prince would have been caught dead in. She laughed when she saw it, and liked him all the better for having done such a thing.

''Disguises,'' he reminded her when she raised an eyebrow.

''Good move,'' she told him approvingly.

She had to wonder what was going on inside his head. He seemed more open, more relaxed than she'd seen him before. If this had been any other man, she would have been certain that they had become very close friends over the last two days. But this wasn't any other man. This was Crown Prince Marco Roseanova of Nabotavia, the most haunted, guarded man she'd ever met. And surely what she'd told him the night before had rankled. If he didn't agree with what she'd said, if he thought she'd been far too impertinent, why didn't he say so? Why didn't he feel the need to put her in her place?

Or did he agree with her? Did he think she was right? Had she started him thinking in ways that might stop him from going ahead with that awful plan to marry Iliana? Could she really have made him think about changing his mind?

No such luck. Mulling it over, she realized that the last thing he'd said to Jordan as they left the hotel room was, "Call me on my cell phone if you hear any news about Princess Iliana."

"As you wish, sir," Jordan had responded, like the faithful servant that he was.

She sighed as she let Marco help her into the passenger's seat. She was still glad she'd told him a few home truths, but she wasn't sure it had made a change. But after all, it was none of her business, was it? She'd been plunked down into this little drama and she was stuck here until it played out. But she was in no way a major player. She had a walk-on role at best and she had better not forget it.

Glancing at Marco's handsome face as they pulled out of the parking structure, she reminded herself of another fact of life. Bit players often fell for the leading man. But though the leading man might flirt with the bit player, he never turned his back on the leading lady in order to walk off with Miss Background Fluff. It just didn't happen. And thinking of that made her feel slightly sick to her stomach.

Why? Biting her lip she realized she would have

to be just as truthful and ruthless with herself as she had been with him the night before. Was she falling for the prince? Was she abandoning her lifelong ability to stay cool, calm and collected in the face of romantic temptation and preparing to hand her heart to a man who didn't want to take it? To be brutally honest, she would have to admit he was a man who *couldn't* take it even if he had actually wanted to.

"In other words," she whispered to herself, "Shannon Harper, you are crazy." Crazy to think this sort of thing would get her anywhere.

"What was that?" he asked, glancing at her as they stopped at a light.

"I was just musing aloud," she told him. "I was thinking about fairy tales and princes and things like that. Things that seem like they're from another time in history. Things you expect to find alive only in your imagination."

He frowned for a moment as though he was thinking over what she'd said, then a thought brought a slight smile to his lips. "Like that unicorn you have on your key chain?" he noted. "I've been meaning to ask you about that. Why does the unicorn have a red rose on his chest?"

"Does he?" She knew he did and she smiled. "Oh, that's right. I don't know. Just a fluke, I guess."

They glanced at each other, gazes meeting. Something magic flashed between them. They both knew the red rose was the symbol of Marco's royal house and they both knew that meant nothing—and yet seemed so rife with possibilities of *something*, that the very air between them seemed to be charged with electricity all of a sudden.

The light changed and the car started forward and Shannon took a deep breath, hoping he couldn't hear the pounding of her heart. Yes, falling for this gorgeous prince would be very easy to do.

Before heading for the museum they took a tour of the city, in daylight this time. With Shannon giving directions and Marco driving the little car, they zipped in and out of neighborhoods doing what almost amounted to a comedy routine with Shannon calling out directions and Marco changing his mind at every corner. Whatever you called it, Shannon thought it was the most fun she'd had in a long time.

They stopped at the same park around a man-made lake where they had walked on the night of the ball. This time they rented a canoe and paddled out into the water, almost tipping enough times to get them both laughing uproariously. The problem was they each had a different idea of how the paddling should be done, and in a canoe, differences of opinion could get ugly. Luckily they retreated to the shore before anyone got too wet.

"My children would love this," Marco said as they sat along the banks to rest and watch the other boaters.

Shannon turned to look at him. She'd forgotten his children. "Where are they?"

"They're in New York right now, with Judith, their grandmother."

"Is that Lorraine's mother?"

"Yes." Reaching into his back pocket, he pulled out a wallet and opened it to show her pictures of two adorable little children. "She's been their major caretaker for the last two years."

Shannon smiled as she looked at the two little tow-heads. "What are their names?"

"Peter is six and Kiki is four."

She looked up into his eyes. She could tell he was a very proud father. "Does your son look like you?"

"Not a bit. But Kiki does." He closed the wallet and put it away.

Shannon looked out at the water. Sunlight shimmered on the little waves made by boaters. "Do you see them very often?"

"Not lately. I'm about to start a major effort to change that. Now that things have settled down in Nabotavia, it should be possible for us to become a more normal family again."

Except for one big glaring hole in that scenario. How could you be a real family when your mother was missing? She frowned, fighting back the sadness, wishing she could push those kinds of thoughts out of her head and keep them out.

"You could be with them right now if you weren't here trying to get this sorted out," she noted.

"Yes. But I've sent for them. They should be here soon."

Shannon brightened. "Great. I hope I get to meet them."

"You like children?" he asked, surprised. Most adults he knew seemed to have a strange aversion for little people like his. Sometimes he wondered if they wouldn't rather just order up progeny who were already grown and skip the messy childhood years.

But she nodded. "I love kids," she said casually.

He thought about that for a few minutes. "You

don't have any children.'' He said it as a statement, not a question, but he was just making sure.

"No. But I've known children. Neighbors and friends and such. And I spent one summer working part-time as an assistant to a nursery school teacher.''

He looked at her curiously. ''You've had so many jobs.''

"A girl has to eat, you know.'' She smiled at him. ''I've also been a dog walker, an usher in a play-house, and for a few days I even drove a cab.''

That was too much and he wasn't sure he believed it. "What were you doing driving a cab?'' he asked skeptically.

She put up a hand, her eyes sparkling with laughter. ''Don't ask. It had to do with pretending to be some-one I wasn't again, when a good friend got sick and was going to be fired if she didn't take her cab out. You don't want to know the details.''

He groaned. This young lady had altogether too little respect for rules. "You're right. I don't want to know.'' But when he looked at her, he wanted to kiss those laughing lips.

The impulse wasn't a new one. He'd been feeling it more and more often and by now he knew it wasn't going to go away. But it was something he had to resist, and he felt confident that he could do that. Shannon was just a traveler passing through this por-tion of his life at the same time he was passing through this portion of hers. They were not destined to be long-term friends.

"Let's walk along the river,'' he suggested, rising and reaching out to help her up. "And while we do, you can tell me about the love of your life.''

She joined him, enjoying the warmth of his hand until he withdrew it. They walked slowly, side by side. "Why do you assume I've had one?"

"Because you are a beautiful woman. I'm sure men have been swarming around you ever since you came out."

She found herself smiling at his characterization of what her life should have been like. The truth was far from his view of reality. And as for "coming out"—that was so far removed from what her teenage years had been like she almost laughed aloud.

"You assume too much," she told him. "I have bad luck with men."

"Surely there has been someone."

He was looking at her expectantly and she began to think she had to tell him something. She thought for a moment, wondering what she could say to him. But there *had* been one man. Turning to him, she smiled.

"I once thought I was in love for a few weeks," she told him. "He was tall and handsome. An international banker."

"Really." He looked interested. "I know quite a few international bankers. What was his name? Maybe I know him."

"Maybe you do." She looked at him sideways. Fat chance. Her international banker was pretty hot stuff but she didn't think he ran in royal circles. "Therefore we will just call him Eric," she added significantly, mainly because that was his name. "He came to Dallas about once a month. The rest of the time he lived in France. When I got a chance to go to Europe on a summer semester in Art History, I thought I would surprise him with a visit. I got his home address in Paris and showed up on his doorstep." She shook her head sadly, but a smile was threatening to break through. "Anticipation began to melt away when his very pregnant wife opened the door and invited me to come in and wait for him. She fed me great coffee and pastries to die for and we talked and talked."

He tried to look sympathetic but it was a pathetic attempt. "And that was the end of Eric's double-dealing ways, I suppose. Did the two of you draw and quarter him when he showed up?"

"Not at all." She gave him a look. "By the time he arrived, I'd settled down and I pretended to be a casual friend who worked with him and had just dropped by to say hello. I didn't think it was fair to break his wife's heart when she was on the verge of having his baby. But *I* certainly lost a bit of my naivete."

They stopped and he leaned against the railing.

"Are you telling me you didn't give him his just desserts at all?" He was gazing at her as though he could hardly believe it.

She shook her head. "I only hope that close call taught him a lesson, too, and that he's a perfect husband and father today."

He groaned. "And you think you've lost your naivete," he murmured cynically, his eyes warm as he looked at her. A breeze caught a strand of her hair and blew it across her eyes. Without thinking he reached out and brushed it back. His gaze drifted down to her soft cheek, her full lips, and the urge to let his fingers rake into her hair and take the back of her head and pull her close was almost overwhelming. He could imagine how she would taste, how warm she would feel, and his body reacted with a speed and force that startled him.

"No," something said in his head, "this is no good."

He turned away, staring out at the horizon. Shannon was the only woman he'd felt this sort of impulse with since Lorraine. He'd thought he was dead in that area, that losing the woman he loved had killed off that side of his life. But Shannon was proving him wrong, and he wasn't sure he liked that.

Suddenly he felt her hand on his arm and he looked down at it, so slender, the fingers pink-tipped.

"What's wrong?" she was asking. "Did I do something...?"

He looked into her eyes and knew he shouldn't have. He could easily get lost in all that sparkling violet beauty. And that was what he wanted to do, to plunge into her warmth and get lost, not to have to think, not to have to deal with anything but the comfort he knew he would find there. Temptation. This was what it meant. He touched her cheek with the palm of his hand and smiled at her.

"You didn't do anything, Shannon," he told her in a low voice. "It's all me."

And he turned from her quickly, before he let himself do anything dumb.

"Let's get going," he said, starting back toward the car. "We need to grab some lunch somewhere. I'm looking forward to this museum trip." Still, somehow he found himself holding her hand as they strolled back over the grass.

* * *

They parked across the street from the museum and Marco twisted his head to scope out the landscape, then groaned. "Damn." He looked at Shannon and shook his head. "The media is lying in wait."

"What? Where?"

Reaching out, he stopped her from being ostentatious about looking by grasping her arm, then directed her gaze.

"Right there." He nodded toward the sidewalk where a young man leaned against the corner of the wrought-iron fence, his camera strategically hidden beneath an open newspaper.

"Ah yes, I see him." She grinned at Marco. "I guess you can smell them a mile away, can't you?"

"I've spent my life avoiding them. You do gain a knack for it." He sighed. "Unfortunately this means we'll have to forgo the museum visit. Maybe some other day."

"What?" She was outraged. "Hey mister, I didn't think royalty would give up that easily."

"Shannon...."

Before he could stop her she'd popped a piece of chewing gum in her mouth and opened the car door, getting out with a flourish that didn't look much like someone trying to avoid attention.

"Shannon," he said again in warning, but she didn't listen. Jamming her huge dark glasses on her nose, she started toward the photographer, her walk an exaggerated strut.

Getting out quickly, he took a step to grab her arm but she gave him a fierce frown and kept on going, leaving him behind to watch her in horror. Stopping traffic, she jaywalked right over to where the man stood. He saw her arriving and did a double take, then watched with relish.

"Hi there," she called out as she got close. "What ch'all waitin' on?"

The photographer was still recovering from witnessing her walk across the street. "Uh, nothing...."

"Sure you are," she said to him flirtatiously. "I can see your camera there. You're with the paper or somethin', ain't cha?" Turning her head she looked up and down the street. "There gonna be a parade here or somethin'?"

The man hiked up his jeans and grinned at her. "Naw," he said, obviously ready to give up his cover story without a fight. "If you really want to know, we got a tip the crown prince of Nabotavia might show up here. They've got this exhibit of Nabotavian art going and him being in town right now and all..."

"A real prince?" She snapped her gum at him. "You gotta be kidding."

"Oh, he's a real prince all right. And he might have Princess Iliana with him. That's the one he's supposed to be marrying, from what they say."

"No kidding?" She looked up and down the street again, as though wondering where they were. "I hope I get to see them."

He grinned at her and looked cocky. "Stick with me and you'll get to see lots of things," he told her.

"Oh, you!" she said, pretending to take a swat at him. Then her face changed, as though she'd just remembered something. "Ohmigod! Wait a minute." She grabbed his arm. "I bet that was him I just saw going into Neiman Marcus on Main Street a few minutes ago. There was this huge crowd gathering and people with cameras like that taking pictures and…''

The photographer looked crestfallen. ''Oh hell. And here I thought I was being so smart hanging out at the museum.'' He thought fast, making mental calculations. ''Neiman Marcus, huh? That's at least three blocks away. I'd better get over there fast.'' He hefted his camera to his shoulder and grimaced at her, motioning to his assistant who was on lookout farther down the street. ''Thanks, sugar. Hey, here, take my card. Give me a call if you see anyone famous, okay?''

''You got it, honey,'' she told him happily, waving his card in the air. ''Good luck. Hope you find that prince guy.''

''Thanks.''

She watched him dash off for the intersection, then turned and gestured toward Marco. He strolled up to her, shaking his head.

''Outrageous,'' he told her, looking down and trying not to grin. ''Does the CIA know about you? You should be listed with the classified weapons of war.''

''I only work for royalty,'' she said pertly. ''And I do it for love.''

She hadn't meant to say that. Her eyes widened with the shock of having said it, and he stared at her for a long moment, as though he couldn't believe it either. ''I do it for love.'' Well, she did, didn't she? In her way. Lifting her chin, she refused to be embarrassed by it.

He grinned, as though he was going to accept it as well. ''You can work for me anytime,'' he said softly, and she gave him a significant look, then slipped her hand into the crook of his arm, enjoying the feel of the hardness and warmth beneath his shirt as they walked into the museum.

Though the exhibit only had five of the works of Havel Dirksonian, they filled the walls, a riot of form and color. Shannon led him into the high-ceilinged room and waited, smiling as she looked from one work to another, basking in the genius of it all.

Marco looked from one work to another also, at first with interest, but eventually with bewilderment. He just didn't get it. The colors were bright. The strokes were huge. But chimpanzees tossing cans of paint at a canvas could have done much the same. Couldn't they?

He looked at Shannon. She was turned toward him, her face full of expectation. Suddenly he wanted very much to please her, to make her face shine with happiness, by telling her how much he loved this stuff. He tried. He smiled at her.

"Well," she coaxed. "What do you think?"

"Uh." His smile seemed brittle all of a sudden. "Yeah, it's really big."

Her face fell in exactly the way he hadn't wanted it to and he felt a stab of regret.

"You hate it."

"No, really, it's very…very…." There were times when words just wouldn't come.

Her face crumpled and she turned away. My God, did she have tears in her eyes? Her shoulders were definitely shaking. He hesitated only a moment, then took her by those shoulders and turned her back, beginning an abject apology, calling himself every sort of ignorant idiot, until he saw her face again. She was laughing. Stung, he pulled his hands away, but she reached for him, taking him by the shirt.

"It is unacceptable for you not to appreciate the art of your own country," she told him firmly. "Come on. We're going to do this by the numbers. I'm going to teach you what this is all about."

He opened his mouth to protest, but the words stopped in his throat. She was right. This was something he needed to know.

"Yes, Miss Harper," he said meekly. "I'm ready to learn."

They spent the rest of the afternoon at it. She walked him through the exhibit slowly, talking about the quality of color, texture, juxtaposition, going through the contrast between emotional response as opposed to intellectual analysis. He watched her, listened to her words, tried hard to see what she saw, and by the end of the session, he really did have a new understanding for what he was looking at.

But more than that, he had a new appreciation for the danger he was in. The more he watched Shannon, the more he wanted to watch her. When she touched him, just a brush of her hand against his skin, he had to stop himself from reaching to take her in his arms. When she leaned close to tell him something confidentially, he had to hold his breath to keep from getting dizzy on her scent. She was becoming his own private intoxicant. And like a dangerous drug, he just wanted more and more of her.

This wasn't right. He shouldn't be reacting this way. But it was getting harder and harder to remember that.

Lorraine, he thought in the familiar way he dialogued with her all the time. *I'm sorry, darling. It's just that...*

His internal voice stopped and he frowned. Lorraine wasn't there. Not the way she usually was. Something flared in his chest, something between fear and panic and regret. Was that the price he would pay for this? Was he going to lose the woman he loved?

Chapter Eight

Back at the hotel, they had a quiet dinner. Marco told Shannon he was going to have to get some paperwork done once the dishes were cleared and she told him she would go watch a movie. But somehow neither thing happened and the two of them ended up before the fireplace, talking on into the night. The shadows grew longer. Jordan came in and turned out some of the lights, signaling the passing time, but they didn't notice him. For the moment, their world was encompassed in the small space between them, and that was all they saw or heard.

Marco told her about his younger years, about the escape from Nabotavia, about the shock of his parents' deaths and of facing the realization that he was the head of the family. He was all of twelve at the time.

"So young to have to grow up," she said softly, her eyes full of compassion for that young boy she could almost see in her mind's eye. It was no wonder he was so serious about so many things. "You didn't get much of a childhood, did you?"

"I didn't have much time to worry about that," he told her gruffly. Except where Lorraine was concerned, he wasn't one to mull over what had happened in the past. The future was his obsession. The future of Nabotavia was a clean slate. So much to do. So much could go wrong. But so much could go right, too, especially with the right guidance. He only prayed he would be the one to provide that and do it well.

"But what about you?" he asked her. "Tell me about your life." His silver-blue gaze skimmed over her slender body, lingering on the way her breasts filled her jersey top. "What's it like to be a girl growing up in Dallas, Texas with a mother who grew up in Nabotavia?"

She laughed. "Not very different from having a mother who grew up in East Texas, I think," she said. She'd noticed the look and she wondered about it. This was new. He was actually letting her see his attraction to her now. Did that mean he was ready to move on it? And if he did, would she let him? Should she?

"Didn't your mother tell you stories of Nabotavia?"

She shook her head. "Not much. She didn't seem to look back on her early days with any great fondness."

Curious. Maybe he was biased, but Nabotavia seemed like such a wonderful place, and if she'd known it before the rebellion, she must have thought so, too. "Why was that do you think?"

She frowned. Odd as it might seem, she'd never really tried to analyze it. Her mother was just the way she was. But if Marco was interested, she would do her best to provide him some answers.

"My mother was a very serious person. She kept her nose to the grindstone and did what she had to do. She wasn't much for stories." But then another thought came to her. "My mother's friend, Jay, told me most of what I know of the country. She's the one who really sparked my interest in it. They used to work together, back in the old country. Jay ended up marrying a very wealthy man and did a lot of traveling, but she always made it a point to visit my mother at least once a year."

She smiled fondly, thinking of her mother's friend. "And she still stops by to this day. I always called her aunt Jay and she's sort of a second mother to me now."

"I'm glad you've had someone. Without her I guess you would be very much alone."

She thought about that for a moment and nodded. "It was Aunt Jay who provided the money to keep my mother in the very nice convalescent home where she spent her last days. That was why I took the job as Iliana. I needed the money to pay Jay back for all my mother's bills that she paid at the time." A faint smile shadowed her face. "It seemed fitting somehow to pretend to be a princess from that part of the world in order to pay back a lady from the same region."

He studied her, looking thoughtful. "So this Jay is Nabotavian also? What is her name?"

"Jay Landreau."

"Landreau." He frowned, staring into space. "Why does that sound familiar?"

"Do you think you know her?"

He thought a moment longer, then shook his head.

"She's a wonderful person, very lively. The exact opposite of my mother! You'd love her." She hesitated, then forged on with a painful subject. "She has a tragedy in her life just like you do. Her beloved daughter died just two years ago. It almost killed her."

He nodded. He knew about that sort of agony. But he was thinking that Jay Landreau was a name he'd heard before and he wondered why he couldn't place it.

Jordan came in to excuse himself. He was retiring for the night and obviously thought they ought to follow his example. Marco teased him and winked at Shannon, making her laugh softly.

Suddenly she wished he weren't a prince, wished it with a sick feeling of hopeless longing that made her gasp. If he were just a man, she would be so in love with him. Even as it was, she was afraid she rather loved him. But she couldn't be *in* love with him, because he could never be hers. He was a prince and that made it impossible. So being *in* love with him would mean she could never be happy. And she couldn't face that.

It was very late and she yawned, stretched, and contemplated going to bed as Jordan had hinted she ought to do. Turning, she found Marco's gaze on her. His eyes were dark as a midnight-blue sky.

"I suppose you're still determined to marry Princess Iliana," she said, feeling a bit wistful.

He nodded slowly. "I have to."

Sighing, she looked away. "It's such a paradox. As the king, you should be able to do whatever you want, but instead, it locks you into having to do things you wouldn't do on your own. Somehow that doesn't seem logical."

"It's about honor, Shannon."

"Honor!" Her head whipped around and she stared at him. "To take such a stupid and destructive step?"

His face hardened and she realized how inappropriate it was to talk to the man who would be king that way. But she didn't have a self-censoring gene, unfortunately, and she was afraid she was going to say what she really thought, regardless.

"You don't understand," he told her coldly. "King Mandrake went out on a limb for me. He didn't have to do it. If he hadn't helped me, I probably wouldn't have been able to free my country and its people. We owe him a lot. And all he asks is this." He shrugged. "I promised. And I have to do it."

An overwhelming sadness swept over her. "Then I wish you luck, Marco. You're certainly going to need it."

Rising, she looked at the door that led to her bedroom. This would be the second night she'd stayed with him here. If Iliana were found tomorrow, it would be her last. How was she going to go back to her lonely life after this?

Funny, but she hadn't even known she was lonely until she'd found herself falling for a prince. She'd never been able to imagine finding a man she could love forever. Now she knew it was possible. She watched him rise and come toward her and every part of her felt a deep longing like she'd never felt before.

"Good night," she said quickly, thinking she'd better get out while the getting was good.

"Shannon…" His hand touched her upper arm, and then his long fingers closed around it, holding her before him. "Wait a minute."

"What is it?" she asked, feeling breathless, and suddenly her heart was beating hard in her throat.

He looked down at her, searched her eyes as if he would find an answer he just had to have. She watched him, hardly daring to breathe, hoping he was going to kiss her. He probably hadn't kissed another woman since… She gasped softly. She would bet the house on this—he hadn't kissed another woman since Lorraine.

Her heart went out to him. For some reason she couldn't explain, even to herself later on when she thought about it, she didn't want the first woman he kissed after Lorraine to be Iliana. It was crazy, but she knew, suddenly, in some completely irrational way, that it had to be her.

Her heart was pounding. The sound filled her ears, filled her head. But she knew she had to do it. Instead of turning and rushing to her bedroom as she knew she ought, she reached for him.

Going up on her toes, sliding her hands around his neck, parting her lips, she caught a quick flash of surprise in his blue eyes, and then her own were closed and she brushed her lips on his in a quick kiss.

It was over almost before it had begun and she found herself back on the ground, his hands on her shoulders firmly holding her away. Looking into his gaze as he drew back, all she saw was a darkness. Aversion? Regret? Guilt? She couldn't tell what it was, but she knew he was disturbed.

"I'm sorry," she said quickly. "But I thought…"

"No," he said quickly, forcing a smile and taking her hand, kissing her fingers. "That was a lovely gesture. Thank you."

Thank you! She didn't want his gratitude. She didn't want polite manners either. She wanted him to grab her and kiss her like he'd never kissed a woman before. She wanted to see passion take hold of his soul and banish discretion. She wanted to feel his heat and hardness, to touch his tongue with hers, to wrap herself around him….

"Shannon," he began, as though he could read her mind and wanted to warn her not to hope for things she couldn't have.

She turned back, looking at him, and all the hurt and longing was in her eyes. Her golden hair seemed to shimmer around her face like an angelic spell and her lips were red and swollen, her body so soft, her skin so warm.

"Oh my God," he said in a sound that was wrenched from his heart. His mind blurred. He couldn't hold on to the rules he'd made for himself, the strict regulation of right and wrong. His famous control slipped, then slid away. The warm affection he had for this woman took over, and not far behind, passion lurked. He reached for her.

She melted into his embrace and he heard a moan and realized it was his own. She felt so right against him, soft as velvet, cool as silk. And she tasted so good, all hot and spicy, like a holiday drink on a cold winter's night. Gathering her closer, he wanted to lift her and carry her to his bed, to wrap her in satin and stake a claim to her, body and soul. He felt her arch into his embrace and he pulled her even closer. His mouth on hers was all hunger, his tongue driving deeper, his hands sliding up to explore her curves.

And then he was blind with desire for her, deaf to anything but her breathing. Too long deprived of the life force she carried, he felt the need for it like an obsession. He couldn't get enough of her. His kisses were deep and hungry and her willing response set his blood on fire.

"Shannon," he murmured, kissing her face and needing to say her name. "Shannon."

She accepted him as though he were a force of nature, meant to be. She'd never felt so alive, so in touch with every sense. She'd had kisses before, known how eager a man could be. But she'd never felt that eagerness in herself before, never known what it was to feel as though she would die if she didn't have his love. Her heart was her gift. Would he accept it?

He knew what she was offering and he knew very well this was no good. He'd known it from the first. He couldn't do this to her, couldn't lead her on this way. Slowly, painfully, he began to reassert control over his own reactions. And when he was strong enough to do it, he pulled away.

"Shannon, I'm...I'm sorry," he muttered as he turned his head so that he couldn't see the shock in her eyes, couldn't see her disappointment. Guilt racked him. Not only had he betrayed Lorraine by doing this, he'd betrayed Shannon as well. Grimacing, he shuddered and then stiffened his shoulders.

"Good night," he said, effectively dismissing her. "I hope you sleep well."

She turned from him blindly, heading in the general direction of her room and hoping she would get into it without making a fool of herself. For some stupid reason a lump rose in her throat. Taking a deep breath, she steadied herself as she entered the room. Then she closed the door.

Shannon slept only fitfully through the night, not really falling into deep sleep until the early morning light, so it was late morning when she heard voices. At first she thought she was dreaming.

"Shhh," a childish voice said. "Kiki! Careful. Don't slam the door."

Marco's children, she realized. It had to be. Lying very still, she kept her eyes closed and listened to them.

"Peter," a little girl lisped. "Peter. Is she a princess?"

"Daddy says no." His young voice was serious and matter-of-fact. "But I think she looks like a princess." His voice brightened. "Hey, maybe she's a secret princess."

"A secret princess," Kiki repeated as though she liked the concept. "Okay."

Shannon risked cracking open her eyes enough to take a look at her audience. The little girl had a pretty face and a cascade of blond curls, while the boy was a bit somber, his darker blond hair cut short and neat.

"How come she doesn't wake up?" Kiki was asking her brother.

Shannon promptly closed her eyes tight again as the little girl half climbed on the bed so that she could lean over her.

"She's sleeping," Peter explained in a loud whisper. "Maybe she's like the story of Sleeping Beauty. Remember that story?"

"Where the prince has to kiss her or she won't wake up?"

"Yeah. That one."

The little girl was leaning so close, Shannon could hear her breathing. This was a pair of darlings. She loved the way they were exploring together, like a true team, searching for adventure. She wanted to open her eyes and say, "Boo," but she held it back.

"Peter, quick, you gotta kiss her." Kiki's voice had an edge of panic. "What if she's stuck in that sleep? You gotta try it."

"I'm not going to kiss her." Peter made a face. It was obvious that the boy-girl thing was a factor in his life and he wasn't sure, but he thought just maybe girls were getting to be icky. "*You* kiss her."

"Okay." Kiki was ever obliging and she leaned down and plunked a wet smack on the secret princess's cheek.

Shannon opened her eyes and looked at them. They stared back.

"Are you a princess?" Kiki whispered at last, her blue eyes wide.

"No," Shannon said calmly. She smiled at them both, then put on a pretend face and changed her voice. "I'm a monster pretending to be a princess!"

She made her move and in one fell swoop, she grabbed them both. "Grrr!" she roared, playing it to the hilt.

Squeals of delight filled the air as she tickled them both. They kicked and laughed and got away and she rose from the bed, chasing them around the room until she'd grabbed them again and fell back on the bed, two wriggling bodies in her control.

Suddenly the door burst open and Marco came rushing in. "What's going on here?" he demanded, looking from one red-faced child to the other, then at Shannon herself.

They all three stared at him, the laughter suspended. "Nothing," they all said in harmony. And that immediately brought back the laughter.

Marco relaxed. He stood and watched for a moment, a slight smile playing on his lips. "From the noise you all made I thought someone was being tortured in here," he said to explain his arrival.

"Of course," Shannon said in a crotchety witch voice. "I'm going to put them both to work in my potato peeling factory. You'll be sorry then, my pretties!"

The children squealed with pretend terror and Shannon hugged them both close, enjoying the feel of their warm, lively bodies. There was something about children of this age that always made her feel life might be worthwhile after all—and so full of potential.

Marco stood watching for another moment. Looking at his children, his heart was full. Looking at Shannon, he felt an emotion he didn't want to accept. She was so beautiful with her hair a wildly tangled mess and her lacy white nightgown billowing around her.

He left the room, closed the door and leaned back against it, his eyes half closed as he savored the scene he'd just witnessed. That picture had brought back memories, regrets, possibilities—possibilities of being a happy family again. How his heart ached for something like that to happen for his children. Hell, he ached to have it for himself.

The memory of the kiss they had shared the night before rose in his mind. He knew he should regret it, but he was finding that hard to do. He thought of Lorraine for a moment, but somehow Shannon's face got in the way. He wanted to kiss her again. He wanted a lot more than that. He groaned softly. It was probably a good thing the children had arrived. It was obvious he needed something besides his guilty conscience to keep his libido in line. A day with children underfoot was just the thing.

Straightening, he recovered his usual calm center of gravity and went back to preparing for his day. He had no time to dwell on the personal. There was work to do.

The morning was somewhat chaotic but to Shannon it was a joy. When she dressed and came out for breakfast, the children ran to her immediately, each wanting her to look at something they had done, or to listen to something they had to say. It was evident they had bonded with her very quickly.

''It seems to be a case of love at first sight,'' Marco said wryly, when he was able to tear her away from them for a moment. "I've never seen them take to anyone so soon after meeting them."

"I told you I was a kid person," she responded. "They're wonderful children."

"*I* like them," he said with some pride, smiling as he looked over to the corner of the room where they were playing with a ball, Peter slowly rolling it to Kiki, who tried hard to catch it, her little face fierce with concentration.

Shannon grinned, then sobered. "You know I told you that my mother's Nabotavian friend Jay Landreau had a daughter who died? The daughter had two children as well, just about the same ages as yours." She shook her head, thinking of them. "I hope they're doing as well as yours are."

He stared at her. That name still rang a bell somewhere in his mind. And now he was getting a very strange feeling about connections and coincidences.

"What sort of family was this Jay Landreau from?" he asked her.

She looked at him, surprised by his question. "I don't know. I've always had the impression that Jay held a rather high-level station in Nabotavia, but she never told me anything about it, or much about her personal life. I think my mother did some sort of secretarial work for her and traveled with her all over Europe. But I know my mother was already living here in Dallas before the rebellion, because I was born here."

That didn't help much. He looked at her, at her beautiful, open face and knew he had no right to ask the question that he contemplated. But something told him the answer to it might help clear a few things up.

"Shannon, who was your father?"

"My father?" She looked more amused than offended by the question. "I don't know. My mother wouldn't ever talk about him. And to tell you the truth, I wasn't ever really interested." That was a lie, though, wasn't it? She'd told herself the lie for years, covering up the fact that she was very much interested, but didn't want to hurt her mother.

"It wasn't Harper?"

"Oh no. Grant Harper married my mother when I was six years old and left her for a younger woman when I was eleven." She smiled thinly. "Another bit of evidence in my mother's book of little black marks against men, you understand."

"I understand." He wanted to take her in his arms and kiss away all the pain he could see in her eyes, much as she tried to hide it. "Do you think you'll ever trust a man?"

Her chin rose. "The right man, maybe." Giving him a flirtatious look, she turned and started toward her room.

He grinned and started to follow her, then looked back at the children and stopped himself.

"Shannon, wait a moment," he said.

She turned back, looking at him expectantly.

"Look, I'm sorry, but Judith dropped the children off this morning and took off for parts unknown. And now the nanny who came with them seems to have disappeared. I'm going to have to go try to find her, but in the meantime, I've got a series of meetings today and…" He paused. "I hate to ask you this, but can you watch them for a while?"

"Sure." Her smile was like the sun coming out on

a cloudy morning. "I'll watch them all day, if you like."

And in the end, that was what she did. The nanny was found, but had been promised the day off and wouldn't be back until late afternoon. So the children were put in Shannon's care for the day.

"I'll take them to the zoo," she said. "Dallas has a wonderful children's zoo with places to play and farm animals to pet. They'll have a great time."

Marco hesitated. "I don't know. I don't think I have any security people available to go with you," he said.

"No problem," she said mischievously. "Why not have Jordan go with us? He'll make the perfect body-guard. No one would dare do anything untoward with him around."

She was only half-serious, but the suggestion was worth it just to see the horror on the valet's mournful face. Marco shook his head and gave her a look, but he couldn't hide his grin and he made a few calls and found a driver and a pair of well-seasoned guards to tag along to the zoo. Jordan was off the hook.

"Oh, Jordan, what do you have against the zoo?" she asked affectionately as she and the children were waiting for the car to arrive.

He looked down his nose at her, though she thought she detected the tiniest twinkle in his eye. "I'm afraid I don't possess the proper togs for such an expedition, Miss," he said.

She laughed. "I'll keep that in mind," she warned him. "Next suggestion will come for something you can wear a tuxedo to."

"Thank you, Miss," he said, bowing.

She had a lovely day with the children and brought them back tired and ready for a long nap. Marco came in as she was tucking them into their beds. He watched for a moment, then she withdrew so that he could give them each a kiss.

As he bent over his son, Peter's arms came around his neck and squeezed tightly. "Daddy?" he whispered sleepily. "Could Shannon be our new mom?"

Marco drew back. "Peter…"

"I know you're supposed to marry some other mom," his little boy said quickly, looking anxious, "but we like this one."

Marco's throat was tight and he cleared it, then kissed his son and stood to leave. "Go to sleep now, Peter. And don't worry. Things will work out for the best."

Peter dutifully closed his eyes and Marco glanced at Kiki, already fast asleep, then left the room, feeling like a heartless criminal. The situation was unexplainable in simple terms to a young boy. Maybe that should tell him something.

He found Shannon flipping through a magazine in the living room. She didn't look any worse for wear despite her long day at the zoo tending to his children. It made him almost angry that she looked so fresh and appealing.

"Jordan has just informed me that I'm obligated to attend a concert tonight," he told her, standing over where she sat. "And I'm expected to bring you with me."

"What?"

He shrugged helplessly. "I'm afraid we're going to have to do it."

She frowned. "Won't we be walking right into the media's glare that way?"

"Of course. But these occasions are set up for exactly that." He sank onto the couch beside her, thinking it over. "You're right, though. We have to be very careful that you don't do anything or look in any way that can later be spotted as a difference from the way Iliana looks or acts."

There was an expression of rebellion on her face that surprised him. He knew without having to be told that she resented having to pretend to be Iliana again.

"I'm sorry, Shannon," he said. "I wouldn't ask you to do this, except…"

"No, it's all right," she said quickly, turning to smile at him. "It's just that…well, it didn't really matter so much before. No one was taking pictures and thinking about the possibility that I might be a phony. But since the ball, with our picture in the paper, and the incident at the ranch, there's going to be much more scrutiny. Do you think it's safe?"

His hand found hers, lacing fingers. He stared at where they were joined. "What if I said I didn't care about that anymore?" he said softly. "What if I told you I just wanted you with me?"

He raised his gaze and met hers, and the joy he saw there made him feel even worse. What was he doing? How could he raise her expectations this way when he knew there was no hope to really fulfill them?

"If you said such a thing, and if you really meant it," she replied in a husky voice. "Then I would have the nerve to tell you…that I think I'm in love."

"Shannon…" He reacted with visceral horror.

"Shhh." She put her finger to his lips. "I said 'think,'" she reminded him with a sad, sweet smile. "Don't worry. I don't expect anything from you. Just let me dream a little, okay?"

"But Shannon..."

Leaning forward quickly, she kissed his lips, then drew back and smiled at him. "Now, tell me. What should I wear to something like that?"

He was breathless at her casual acceptance of her own feelings as opposed to his inability to reciprocate. There was no anger, no bitterness in her. She'd decided she loved him, and knew it wasn't going to go anywhere. But that was just the way things were.

Staring at her, he had a hard time reconciling her independent spirit, her willingness to confront truths he himself tried to avoid, with her seeming acceptance of fate. How could those two strains exist side by side this way? And suddenly he knew what she was—a wonderful and delightfully complex puzzle that would take some man years and years to unravel. And he knew something else—he wished very much that the man who got to make that trip could be him.

But she was looking at him expectantly, awaiting an answer to her question. What should she wear?

"Don't worry about that," he said distractedly. "Jordan's already put a suitable gown in your room."

She shrugged and threw out her hands. "Of course. I should have known." She rose from the couch. "I'd better go start getting ready. I'm going to need to wash my hair. Otherwise, I'm afraid I might end up with zoo smells at the concert. And that would never do!"

"Shannon." He rose, too, regret in his eyes.

She shook her head. "Don't think twice," she told him. "The way I feel about you is my problem, not yours." She gave him a dazzling smile. "I just had to tell you, that's all." She turned and hurried off to her room.

He stood watching her go. Something twisted in his chest and he wasn't sure what it was. Maybe your heart is finally defrosting, a voice in his head said with a touch of sarcasm. He frowned, pushing the palm of his hand into his chest and wincing. Maybe that really was it. How the hell did he know?

"Princess Iliana has been found." Marco folded his cell phone and put it into his breast pocket.

"Really?" Shannon looked out the limousine window, her heart sinking. He looked happy with the news, so why did it feel like her world was crashing down around her ears? "Where is she?"

"In Europe, believe it or not. They found her playing at the tables in Monte Carlo." He sighed, stretching out his long legs. "I've got some agents bringing her back to Dallas."

She hesitated, wondering why he didn't just go to Europe to see her. After all, they would be closer to her father and to Nabotavia as well. But she stopped herself before she brought it up. The last thing in the world she wanted to do was to encourage him in this endeavor.

The limousine rolled to a stop in front of the concert hall and Marco helped her from the car. They were both dressed beautifully and the waiting bit of a crowd murmured in appreciation.

"Shall we?" he said. He presented his arm and she

took it, reminding herself to be royal, holding her head high. It was amazing to be the center of attention this way. Once inside and seated, every direction she looked in, all she saw were the round lenses of binoculars pointed her way. It was like being in a room full of giant insects. Very curious insects.

The music was gorgeous, if a bit heavy at times, and for a while she forgot everything else as she lost herself in it. But when she looked to her right and saw Marco's classical profile, her heart fluttered in her chest and she began to think again of how little time they had left together.

At the intermission he escorted her into the private meeting room where refreshments were being served. She was introduced to one Nabotavian after another, some of whom she'd seen at the ball a few nights before, some who were completely new to her.

And all the time, Marco watched her with a growing sense of pride. She was gracious, regal, beautiful. She was perfect. If only he deserved her.

They went back to their seats and just as the lights went down, he happened to look up and there was Judith, Lorraine's mother, disappearing through the doors at the top of the far aisle. She was laughing, with a circle of friends around her, and he knew she was probably escaping to a more cheerful party somewhere.

Turning back, he noticed that Shannon was staring in the same direction, looking puzzled.

"What is it?" he asked her.

She leaned close to whisper, as the performance had resumed. "For just a moment, I thought I saw my friend Jay Landreau. But I must have been mistaken.''

She went back to watching the musicians, but Marco sat as still as though he'd been turned to stone. It finally sank in, but somehow he'd known it all along, hadn't he? Could Jay Landreau and Judith be the same person? It was all beginning to make a horrible sort of sense.

Chapter Nine

The ride back in the limousine was a quiet one. Marco was deep in his own thoughts and Shannon was trying to keep depression at bay. This was it, she knew. The dream was over. The real Iliana was on her way back and the faker had to get out of town before it was too late.

"High noon," she murmured. "Showdown at the corral."

"What was that?" He turned to look at her.

She shook her head. "Nothing. Just muttering incoherently. I do that sometimes."

She thought he would be impatient with her, but he almost smiled. "What's wrong?" he asked her simply, reaching out to take her hand in his.

She looked at him in surprise.

"I'm starting to miss you already," she told him, deciding to be honest.

"Miss me?" He frowned. "Why?"

"Iliana is on her way back. This is obviously it. I'm going to be yesterday's news in a very short time."

He stared at her for a long moment, tightening his hand on hers. "That's ridiculous. You're not going anywhere."

She begged to differ. "Sorry, but I'm not sticking around to pick up table scraps," she said tartly, though there was a catch in her voice.

He heard it and frowned, shaking his head. "Shannon," he said softly, his gaze tracing the outline of her face, then her neck, "sometimes you say the most absurd things."

She looked up and tried to smile, and the next thing she knew she was being pulled into his arms.

"Wait!" she said.

"Why?" He pulled her closer.

"The driver!"

"Can't see a thing. The barrier is up."

"But, wait…."

He looked down at her, bemused. "Why?"

"Because…. I don't know…."

He searched her eyes for answers and all he saw was fear. It wasn't the driver she was afraid of. She was thinking about what was soon to happen. Maybe he ought to think about it, too. But thinking only brought up the confusion that was swirling inside him. Confusion fueled uncertainty, and he didn't like uncertainty. He knew what he wanted right now. He wanted Shannon. And he was sick of trying to deny it.

Slowly he lowered his face to hers and began dropping quick kisses on the line from her ear along her neck, sending sensations like sparks all down inside her, making her moan softly. Raising his head to look at her, his smoldering gaze caressed her mouth. "Shannon, I've been wanting to kiss you for about as long as I've known you."

"Really?" she said a little breathlessly, dying to feel that kiss. "But last night…"

"I was trying to be good last night," he murmured, his lips lowering toward hers as he pulled her even closer. "Tonight I feel a little bad."

"Mmmm…" she whispered, and then she couldn't say any more because his mouth was taking hers and she felt herself open like a flower to the sun.

Smooth as silk, hot as a summer fire, scary as a roller-coaster ride. He was all that and much, much more. He tasted like thick buttery caramel. Well, not really, but the effect was the same—the sort of delicious that made her eyes roll back in her head. She wanted more, needed more, and as his tongue probed deeper into her mouth, she arched her body into his, wanting to feel his hard flesh against every body part she could manage.

"Shannon," he murmured against her lips. "You feel like heaven."

She ached for him. Places she had never heard from before were clamoring for attention, quivering with anticipation, twisting with the need to feel him take her in a serious embrace.

She reached up and sank her fingers into his thick hair, pulling her body tightly against his, feeling his heart racing against her breasts, feeling her own heart pounding like surf against a stormy beach. And from deep inside her came a call, a hunger, a driving need like she'd never felt before. She wanted this man like she'd never wanted any other. Why oh why did it have to be him?

He pressed his face to hers, rubbing softly, sliding against her like a cat, whispering something soft. She couldn't understand the words but she knew what he was saying. And she answered with soft sounds that said the same thing.

The car was slowing. They were entering the hotel parking structure, making for the back entrance where they wouldn't be seen arriving. Sighing with regret, Shannon began the slow process of disentangling herself from his lovely embrace.

"People make love in the backs of limousines, don't they?" she said softly.

He smiled down at her. "All the time."

She sighed. "But we won't do that." She said it firmly. She'd made up her mind, much as she might regret it.

"No," he agreed, letting her go, and his own regret was plain on his face and in his voice. "We won't."

The car came to a stop and the driver asked for instructions. Marco told him they were ready to disembark and he turned off the engine and came around to open the door for them.

"You mean so much to me, Marco," she told him, as she gathered her skirt and prepared to get out. "I don't think I will ever forget you."

"Shannon, I..." he started softly, his eyes burning in the shadows.

But she was already leaving the limousine.

They rode the elevator in silence, but she couldn't stop looking into his beautiful eyes. Once back in the suite, they looked in on the sleeping children, and then Shannon said good-night. He stopped her and dropped a quick kiss on her lips.

"Good night," he said softly, and she nodded, knowing they weren't going to continue what they had begun in the limousine, not with the children here. She turned to go, hoping to hold back her tears until she was alone.

"Wait, Shannon," he said softly, but she didn't stop. There was no point to it. Closing the door to her bedroom, she closed her eyes and let the tears flow.

Shannon was gone. The children were the first to find out. They came running in to Marco's room, their faces filled with worry. Marco came quickly, just to be sure. Her bed was neatly made and three notes were pinned to the pillow, one to each of the children and one to him.

The notes to Peter and Kiki were full of love and fun and promises. The note to him was short and to the point.

"Thanks. It's been fun. Lots of luck in your new life as king. Love, Shannon."

His chest felt tight and his heart was pounding. He'd only known her for a few days, and yet somehow he couldn't imagine life without her now. Mind racing, he called downstairs to see if he could stop her, but she was long gone. He called the restaurant, her little house in the suburbs, the princess's ranch— no one had seen her. In the midst of all this he got a call telling him Iliana had escaped from the guards he'd sent, but he didn't really care. He had to find Shannon. The only person left to talk to was Judith.

Marco found her hiding out at another hotel. Though time consuming, it wasn't difficult. There were only so many luxury hotels in town and he knew darn well she wasn't going to go economy. She came to the telephone quickly enough and agreed to come over to his hotel room later in the afternoon. He had the nanny take the children shopping and to the park. And then he waited.

Judith arrived right on time. She was tall and stately and dressed in an expensive wool suit. Though not technically royal, she'd swum in royal circles all her life. Judith knew everyone. As Lorraine's mother, she'd been a big part of Marco's life for many years and there was a large reservoir of affection between the two of them. She and Marco met with the usual hugs and brushing of lips. She asked after the children and he told her where they were. They chatted about inconsequential items. Then he settled back on the couch and looked at her sitting across from him in an armchair, a slight smile playing on his lips, but no humor in his eyes.

"Tell me, Judith, does the name Jay Landreau mean anything to you?"

She started, but quickly smiled to cover it up. "Why, yes it does."

"I thought it might." His eyes narrowed. "A good friend of yours perhaps?"

Her smile broadened. "Rather."

He stared at her for a long moment, and when she didn't elaborate, he leaned forward and fixed her with a glare. "Come clean, you wicked woman," he said coldly. "What have you done here?"

She gave him a long-suffering look. "Anything I've done was for your own good."

He barely stopped himself from rolling his eyes. "You are Jay Landreau, aren't you?"

She smiled. "Landreau was my maiden name long ago. And as a child, I was always called Jay. Short for Judith."

He shook his head, glaring at her. She had always claimed she wouldn't stand by and see him marry Iliana, but he had never expected anything like this from a woman he thought he knew so well. He was furious with her. But at the same time, he needed something from her. Where, after all, was Shannon?

Shannon was, at that very moment, slipping back into the hotel room as quietly as possible. She didn't have a key, but she'd seen a maid who recognized her in the hall and let her in, knowing she'd been staying there. She was hoping to avoid Marco, but find the children here with the nanny, as she knew that had been the plan for the afternoon the last she'd heard.

The way she'd left had been torturing her all day. It was one thing to leave a terse not for Marco, it was quite another to skip out on the children without saying a real goodbye. So she'd come back to do just that.

But now that she was inside, she hesitated in the entryway. Instead of the voices of Kiki and Peter, she heard another voice that was even more familiar.

"Jay?" she whispered to herself, frowning. Then joy opened her heart. It was her old friend! She took a step toward the doorway, only to stop again as she realized how strange this was. And in that moment, she heard Marco's voice and she bit her lip, feeling off balance, as though she'd stepped into some mirrored wonderland. Leaning against the wall, she listened intently, wanting to get the lay of the land before bursting in on them.

"Shannon's mother was in many ways my best friend," Jay's voice was saying. "Nina was in the secretarial pool at my father's organization when I found her. I pulled her out and made her my secretary and public relations assistant. She was very good at it and we became close friends. I took her with me everywhere I went."

Shannon frowned, wondering why they were talking about her mother, and as Marco spoke it began to dawn on her that what they were discussing was going to change her life.

"One of those places was King Mandrake's castle, wasn't it?" he said, his voice deep with significance.

Shannon held her breath, waiting for Jay's reply, instinctively knowing the answer was going to be important, although she wasn't really sure why.

"Yes," Jay said. "Yes, he was in his prime in those days. Quite a ladies' man."

There was a long pause but Shannon still didn't breathe. Finally Marco spoke again.

"Mandrake is Shannon's father, isn't he?"

At first Shannon couldn't comprehend the words. She softly let her breath out and took another, but even as Jay spoke again, she wasn't sure of what she was hearing.

"I believe so. Though I've never seen the DNA proof."

Marco's laugh was short and bitter sounding. "All you have to do is look at her."

"Yes."

Shannon's mind was a blur. Still leaning against the wall, she slowly descended until she was sitting on the floor, staring dumbly into space. King Mandrake's daughter? No, she'd just been pretending. Didn't they understand? But slowly the truth was filtering in through her protective denial. King Mandrake's daughter. Of course. Once she heard that, all the pieces of her life that had seemed so discordant began to fall into place.

They went on talking, but she barely heard what they were saying. Her mind was full of swirling thoughts and her heart was pounding so loudly, she had to wonder if she were having an attack. Closing her eyes, she let her head fall back against the wall and tried to concentrate on what was being revealed in the next room.

"Her mother purposefully kept her here in Dallas, away from anything to do with Nabotavia or Alovitia," Jay was saying. "Though there is a small immigrant community here, she made sure Shannon didn't have any contact with them. She didn't want her daughter to come up against the sorts of temptations she had, and to suffer the same consequences and pain. The commoner falling in love with the king." She waved a hand in the air. "And yet, here you are repeating history."

Marco's voice was soft but harsh. "Yes, but that's your fault, isn't it?"

"Of course. Yet it seems like destiny to me."

"Destiny? To repeat the heartbreak?"

"No. It doesn't have to be that way at all." Rising, the handsome older woman came and sat beside him, taking up his hand. "This time," she said with a loving light in her eyes, "it's for you to make it right."

He stared at her, stared into her eyes. "Lorraine…"

"Lorraine loved you with all her heart and you loved her the same way. When you lost her, you almost lost your will to live."

"If it hadn't been for the children," he murmured, agreeing to a certain extent.

She nodded. "But my sweet daughter is out of our reach now. And you need a woman in your life."

He winced. Why couldn't she understand? "I'm not just a man, Judith. I'm going to be a king. My people must come first."

"Yes. And that is why Shannon should be your queen." She threw down his hand and turned away, fretting. "Oh, Marco, you know very well that Iliana is not the queen for Nabotavia. She's not the wife for you, nor the mother for your children. Just because her father saw an opportunity to give her one more chance at redemption, through your good graces, doesn't mean you have to fall for it."

"I made a promise."

The look on Judith's face showed what she thought of such promises. "Break it."

"I can't."

Judith stared at him for a moment, then turned away, frustrated.

"Shannon is a very brave woman you know. She's brave enough to confront you. She's brave enough to confront the world if she needs to. She's brave enough to be a queen.''

He knew that. Shannon's character wasn't the element in question here. ''Tell me how you got Shannon involved in all this.''

She sighed. ''I've known Shannon since she was a baby. I helped Nina find a home here in Dallas. I tried to help her financially in any way I could, though she was always determined not to take anything from me.''

''But she let you be a part of her life, even though you'd helped to ruin hers.''

''Please, Marco, so judgmental.'' She shook her head. ''I will admit I felt a certain amount of guilt in the matter. But I also loved Nina like a sister. And Shannon…'' She smiled. ''What a delight Shannon is. I thought about trying to get the two of you together before Iliana even entered the picture. After all, she's in many ways a second daughter to me.''

''So you got her hired to pretend to be Iliana.''

''Actually you can't entirely blame that on me. When I heard Greta and Freddy were in town trying to keep Iliana in line—now there's a hopeless task! Anyway, I'd known them in Alovitia, you know, they were always hanging around the court, trying to be useful in order to curry favor with the king. So I told them about her, not her lineage, but the fact that she looked a lot like Iliana. And it was their idea to have her play the part.''

''But you didn't discourage it.''

''Not at all. I thought it a lovely way for you to meet her. I knew if I tried to bring you together in any overt way you would both reject the idea. She's almost as stubborn as you, you know.''

He grimaced, feeling tortured. ''To what end, Judith? I still have to marry Iliana.''

She shook her head, tragedy lining her face. ''Don't you understand, Marco? You are in charge now. You make the rules.''

He rose from the couch, running his fingers through his thick hair, and that was when he saw Shannon standing in the doorway, looking as though she'd been hit by a bus.

''Shannon!'' He went to her, but she shook her head, putting him off with a look.

''Shannon, darling,'' Judith said, but she stayed where she was and looked wary.

Shannon stared at them one at a time. ''So I'm the illegitimate daughter of King Mandrake?'' she asked softly. ''Is that the way it is?''

Judith sighed. ''Darling, I'm so sorry you had to hear it this way.''

Marco stood very still and didn't say anything, but the compassion in his blue eyes spoke volumes.

''I feel as though my entire life has been a lie,'' she said. She was determined not to cry. There would be plenty of tears in her future. She knew that very well. But she wouldn't cry in front of them.

''Oh Shannon, dear, don't let yourself get maudlin. Think of it as a living fairy tale.''

She shook her head. ''More like a living nightmare,'' she said. ''Do you think this is a good thing? Because I don't.'' She lifted her chin and stared into her old friend's gaze. ''Royalty. Aristocracy.'' She said the names as though they were abhorrent to her.

"You people are exactly what my mother always said. You manipulate others as though they are pieces on a chessboard. You live up in the clouds and think you're better than everyone else. You trample on the hopes and dreams of people, just because you can."

"Shannon, please…" Marco took a step toward her but she warded him off with a glare.

"I already said goodbye to you, Marco. And I meant it. I just came back to say goodbye to the children. Please tell them I love them." She shook her head, her violet eyes huge with tragedy. "Go on with your plans," she said coldly. "But leave me out of your royal schemes. I don't want any part of them."

Turning on her heel, she left the room. Marco started to go after her, but then he stopped and stared at the door she'd just slammed in his face. She'd looked as though her heart was broken. But damn it, so was his.

"I'll talk to her," Judith was saying. "Don't worry, she'll get over it. I'll explain everything and she'll come around."

But Marco hardly heard her. His romantic interlude with the counterfeit princess was over and he knew it.

That night, alone in his bedroom, he took out the photograph of Lorraine that he always carried with him. She looked young and loving and lovely. She would always look that way. For years she'd filled his heart and left room for very little else, except the children. How had Shannon managed to squeeze her way in as well?

"Lorraine," he whispered, tracing her cheek with his finger. "I'm sorry."

He'd never thought he would feel anything for another woman. Shannon had shown him he was wrong. But as he stared at the picture, he realized that his affection for Shannon had nothing to do with Lorraine. Nothing would ever come between him and his first wife. She was a part of him and always would be. So how was there so much room for Shannon? Maybe his heart had grown bigger. Could that be it?

He knew it was just his imagination, but he could have sworn he saw Lorraine smile.

The next day, gloom reigned. Marco ordered lunch and had the children at the table with him, but they were cranky and only wanted to know where Shannon was. He looked at their sad faces and saw his own pale and drawn visage in the mirror. They were all missing her, and it wasn't fun at all.

Even Jordan seemed to be down.

"All right, Jordan," Marco said after he'd put the children to bed. "You are bursting at the seams, waiting to give me the benefit of your wise counsel. Get it over with."

"Sir?"

"Don't be coy. I'm sure you have something to say. Out with it."

"Yes, sir, actually, I do." Clearing his throat, he struck a pose, much like a nineteenth-century orator. "A man's word of honor is very important, sir."

"Indeed it is."

"And I would never, never advise that you break your word."

"Of course not."

"Especially since you are about to become a monarch and as such, the exemplar for your people, not to mention your children.''

''Yes.''

''However...''

''Ah, I was hoping there was going to be a 'however.'''

''Rigidity in any form is a characteristic to be treated with care and only used sparingly. And judgement is always valuable.''

''Of course.''

''It would be a very sad thing to make an enemy of King Mandrake. He is a powerful man and could do Nabotavia much harm.''

''Yes.''

''But there are worse things.''

Marco nodded, a slight smile playing on his lips. ''I think I am beginning to get your drift, Jordan. And I am beginning to think that perhaps I agree.''

''Sir.''

He frowned for a moment, then snapped his fingers. ''Pack up our bags, Jordan. We're going to Europe.''

''So suddenly, sir?''

''Yes. I have some loose ends to tie up. Things to do, people to see.''

''Very well, sir. It will be my pleasure.''

Chapter Ten

Shannon could hardly contain herself. This was a day she'd dreamed of all her life. She was riding down the main street in Kalavia, the capital city of Nabotavia. The shops that lined the cobblestone street were adorably quaint, the people curious and happy looking, the celebratory atmosphere exciting. And high above it all, on a hill overlooking the city, stood the ancient spires of Red Rose Castle, family seat of the Roseanovas who had ruled Nabotavia for hundreds of years.

"Are you ready for this?" Jay asked, smiling at her from the other side of the limousine.

Shannon smiled back. It would always be "Jay" to her, no matter what others called her mother's old friend. Without Jay, none of this would be happening. There were times she pinched herself anyway, sure that it was a dream she would wake from. But today it seemed to be her reality.

She had come to Nabotavia to take a position as the assistant to the head curator of the Nabotavian Art Museum. It was supposed to be on-the-job training, but it was still a fabulous opportunity for someone who had barely earned her Master's. She was going to learn everything there was to managing a national art collection, and everything there was to renovating a museum system that had fallen on hard times over the last twenty years.

"You'll be the head curator yourself in no time," Jay had assured her. "Old Mr. Potvin will be a gold mine of advice, but he's a little too tired to hang on much longer. As his assistant, you'll be in perfect position to take over."

"Oh, don't say that."

"Of course I'll say it. That's what this job is all about, readying you for that position."

"Yes, but…" Was that really what she wanted? She supposed it was what she'd been aiming at all along—the crowning ambition of her life, so to speak. And yet, there was something else she wanted more, something she could never have.

She'd thought she would forget Crown Prince Marco quickly. After all, their romance had been short and bittersweet. Finding out about her heritage, about how Jay had manipulated things, had confused and infuriated her. She'd agonized over it for days and it had taken time before she could let Jay back into her life. But her old friend had helped her come to terms with it. She'd stayed in Dallas and coaxed Shannon into accepting her friendship again, then made her see that she could use her new circumstances to her advantage. Even now she sometimes had moments where her stomach knotted up painfully and the feelings of dread came back to her. But she had a life to live and a career to build.

She'd agonized over taking this offer. It was a wonderful opportunity. But did she really want to be where she would have to see Marco and Iliana together every day of her life? That was the question. She would see if she could stand it.

She hadn't seen him since that day in the hotel room in Dallas, the day her world had changed. It had taken some time to get used to the fact that she was tied to Alovitia and Nabotavia in ways even deeper than she'd ever dreamed, but once she learned to deal with it, she also had to confront the fact that Marco would be in her world, one way or another. She couldn't hide from him. She had seen the children. Jay had made sure of that. And her relationship with them had only grown. She was looking forward to seeing them again very soon.

But right now her mind was on seeing Marco again. She was going to be cool, calm and collected. She would treat him like an old close friend. No, she would treat him like the head of state that he was. No, maybe she would act as though she hardly remembered who he was....

"Oh hell, I'll do whatever comes naturally!"

They arrived at the museum, a large, imposing structure built in the seventeenth century.

"You'll be presented to the museum board in the main meeting room," she was told by the official who greeted her. "Please come this way."

"Who's on the board?" she asked, waving to Jay and hurrying to follow the young man.

"The entire royal family," he responded, and she blanched.

Oh no! She wasn't ready to face Marco yet, much less his relatives. Panic swept over her as she madly tried to think of an excuse to skip the meeting. But it was too late.

"Miss Shannon Harper, assistant to the curator," her guide announced as he opened the door to a high-ceilinged room.

Taking a deep breath, she stepped in and put on a smile, expecting to see a room full of people. But there was only one, a very pretty young woman with honey-blond hair and a warm, welcoming smile.

"There you are," she said, coming forward with her hand outstretched. "I'm so pleased to meet you. I'm Princess Karina, the youngest of the Roseanova clan. I understand you've only met Marco so far."

"Yes," she said hesitantly, thrown off by the princess's friendly nature. "We met in Dallas."

Karina nodded wisely. "I've heard all about it," she said, her eyes sparkling. "I only wish I'd been there to see him when he realized you weren't really Princess Iliana." She giggled. "He's always so dignified and sure of himself. It would have been a kick to see him dumbfounded like that."

"Well, I have to tell you, he managed to maintain that dignity through it all," Shannon responded, liking this young woman immensely already.

"Oh no." She shook her head in mock despair. "But maybe you're just being diplomatic," she added hopefully.

Before Shannon had time to answer, she was off on another subject.

"I'm sure we'll be working together a lot. I'm going to take charge of the history archives. The entire field has been completely ignored for a long time and some of the ancient texts have actually been allowed to fall apart. I'm going to be scouring the continent, looking for copies of the histories we will need to get back up to date."

A pair of handsome men came into the room and Karina called them over. "This is my husband, Jack Santini," she said as the two of them shook hands. "And this disreputable-looking cutie is my brother, Prince Damian."

Damian was a bit disheveled, but he explained that away immediately. "On our way over, Sara saw a cat up a tree and volunteered me to climb up and save it. She's busy finding the owner right now."

The others laughed, but he was squinting at Shannon. "So this is the woman Marco handpicked to take over as curator when old Mr. Potvin retires," he said. "I'm pleased to meet you."

She flushed, not sure what to make of what he'd said. Marco had handpicked her? This was news. At least, now she knew he wouldn't be shocked to see her here.

Sara waved as she entered and took her seat, her long blond hair shining like silver. A young couple came in, so deeply involved in looking lovingly into each other's eyes that they seemed oblivious to all around them.

"That's my brother Prince Garth and that redhead is my distant cousin, Princess Tianna, of the White Rose Roseanovas," Karina whispered as the meeting was being unsuccessfully called to order by the el-

derly curator. "They've been betrothed since childhood, but resisted getting married until they fell in
love. Can you imagine?"

"The best-laid plans of mice and men," Shannon
quoted with a grin.

"Exactly," Karina answered, laughing at her. She
squeezed her hand. "I can tell we're going to be great
friends."

An older man and woman entered the room, the
older man looking mild and meek, the woman looking
as though she felt she had to direct his every move.

"That's my aunt and uncle, the duke and duchess
of Gavini," Karina said. "You'll love him and admire her. She can be a big help if you have a problem
with anyone."

Shannon nodded. She knew the type. But she was
getting more and more nervous. Where was Marco?

She took a seat at the table right next to Karina.
Mr. Potvin finally had the attention of the others.

"I've called you here in order that we…"

"Wait," the older woman said, rising from her
place and frowning around the room. "Where is
Marco? What can have gotten into him? He knew we
were having a meeting."

"Crown Prince Marco contacted me and excused
himself," Mr. Potvin told her rather peevishly. "May
I please continue?"

"Well certainly," the duchess said, giving him a
look. "It's your meeting. Do what you like."

"Thank you."

The two of them glared at each other and the rest
of the assembly tried to smother their grins. Karina

stood up with the obvious intention of calming the waters.

"I think—"

"Hey! She claims she thinks," Garth teased.

There were snickers but Karina glared at him. "As the only married woman in the family, I consider myself the elder stateswoman," she began.

But the duchess took immediate offense, rising quickly. "Please! I'm not ready to relinquish that role quite yet," she stated emphatically.

"I have an idea. Why don't the two of you arm wrestle for it?" Damian suggested.

There were groans all around and Shannon laughed softly. She could tell meetings with this bunch were going to be lively. Mr. Potvin had his hands full. And someday, she was supposed to take over. She shuddered. As the man went on with the meeting, she looked around, feeling as though she were in the twilight zone. How had this happened? It was so strange. He introduced her to the assembly and they all seemed very welcoming. And then the meeting was over.

She stayed behind, talking to Karina, and then they were all gone and she was all alone. Turning to look at the medieval room, she smiled with the pleasure of being there and began putting her papers away in her briefcase. This was an exciting new adventure she was embarking on.

Suddenly she had the sense that someone else was in the room and she turned. Marco stood in the doorway. She stared at him, her heart an open book. It had been two months since she'd last seen him in person, but she'd kept a picture of him in her mind and he was always in her dreams.

"Hello," he said, coming slowly toward her, his blue eyes dark in the shadows.

"Hello," she said back, and she smiled, reveling in the sight of him. All her plans to maintain a cool exterior flew out the window. What did she care if he knew? She loved him with all her heart and he might as well know it.

But she expected him to stop a few feet away and nod in a friendly manner, perhaps extend his hand. Instead, he just kept coming. Her eyes widened as his arms swept around her and he pulled her up close, burying his face in her hair.

"Oh!" she cried, wrapping her arms around his neck and melting against his wonderful body. "What are you doing?"

"Welcoming you to Nabotavia," he murmured, rubbing his cheek against hers and finding her lips. "We're friendly people, you know." His mouth slanted against hers, and then his kiss deepened and she gasped, greedy to feel his tongue. His hands slipped beneath the fabric of her shirt and slid up her back, then down beneath the waistline of her skirt, setting her flesh on fire.

"Marco," she protested groggily. Her mind was jumbled with contradictory reactions and she couldn't think straight. "I don't understand...."

"There's only one thing you need to understand right now," he murmured very close to her ear. "I need you. We belong together."

"But what about Princess Iliana?"

He smiled down at her and said, "I suppose you've

heard that King Mandrake is threatening war against us.''

"No! What happened?''

He shrugged. "He is taking it very hard that I have refused to marry Iliana.''

Her heart felt as though it might burst from her chest. She gasped. "You broke the engagement?''

"Yes.''

"But…why?''

He gave her a quizzical look, as though she ought to know darn well why, then smiled. "Jordan's advice,'' he said teasingly.

"Ah. Of course.'' She knew he was joking but her mind was still too confused to get the joke right now. He wasn't marrying Iliana. He was declaring the need to have Shannon Harper in his life instead. Did that mean…? She didn't dare complete that thought. Instead, she tried to smile. "You always do take Jordan's advice on everything. I should have known.''

"Absolutely.'' He touched her cheek lovingly with the flat of his hand, as though he couldn't get over how good she looked. Then he looked serious for a moment. "Actually it was because I had decided I needed someone more appropriate to be queen of this country.''

She blinked, suddenly short of breath. Was he really hinting at what she thought he was hinting at? "So…'' She shrugged and searched his gaze, her heart beating like a wild thing. "Who…who do you have in mind?''

He shook his head as though he couldn't believe she didn't know by now. "Oh, I don't know,'' he said teasingly. "I'm choosing from a very small pool of candidates.'' He pretended to look innocent. ''Museum curators. I've decided I need a woman who can bring back the culture in this broken land.''

Okay, she got it now. There was very little doubt. And she wasn't going to let him think he could get away with teasing her without a little teasing back. ''Fascinating,'' she said, her eyes smiling at him. ''You know, I just happen to know an art historian who might be interested.''

He shook his head. ''Sorry. I've already got one all picked out.''

''Oh.'' She put on a crestfallen look. ''Who might that be?''

He pulled her back into his arms. ''You don't really have to ask, do you?'' he said gruffly, kissing her nose, her forehead, her upper lip. He stared down at her, suddenly quite serious. ''Shannon Harper, I love you.''

Her heart was full. Tears rimmed her eyes. ''Marco Roseanova, I love you, too.''

His smile was full of emotion. ''I've thought about you every minute of every day. I don't know how you could have changed my life in such a short time, but you did. You captured my heart.''

His kiss was deep and full of an emotion she knew she would never get enough of. She kissed him back hungrily, greedy to taste him, determined to let him know how much she cared. He pulled back and laughed at her.

''We need to go to dinner right away,'' he said.

''We do?''

''Yes. I'm going to ask you to marry me after dessert.''

She laughed at him. "Why not now?"

He looked as though that were a completely new idea to him. "All right." He stood at attention and though he wore a beautifully tailored business suit, suddenly he could have been attired in his gorgeous uniform with the braid and medals. Clicking his heels together, he put a hand over his heart and stared at her imperiously.

"Shannon Harper, I, Crown Prince Marco of the Royal House of the Red Rose of Nabotavia request that you do me the honor of consenting to be my bride."

She was still laughing, charmed by the whole routine. "Say that in English," she commanded. "I want to make sure I heard you right."

He dropped with graceful panache to one knee and took her hand in his, his imperious manner evaporating and his love shining in his eyes. "My darling and beautiful Shannon, will you marry me?"

"Yes! Oh yes!"

"And my children…?" he asked, rising again.

"I'll marry them, too. I love them almost as much as I love you." She smiled at him through tears of joy. "In time, maybe more."

"Maybe," he agreed, holding her hand to his heart. "I'm not going to be easy to live with."

"What man is?" she asked, echoing her upbringing. And then she went into his arms, a place she was never going to leave again.

Epilogue

"Think fairy tales," Jay told her when she asked what the combined weddings and coronation would be like. "Think books with gold embossed pages and carriages and crowns."

"And the entire populace dancing in the streets for three days," Tianna added, popping a grape into her mouth.

The royal family was sitting in the rose garden, snacking on fresh fruit and basking in the sunlight of a mild winter afternoon.

"Think wine, women and song," Marco provided.

"Not a bit of it," Jay protested. "At least not where you're concerned."

"More like, think ermine, velvet and long, long boring ceremonies," Karina suggested.

"I think I prefer the wine, women and song," Marco said with a groan.

The others laughed, but when his gaze met Shannon's, he smiled at her in a way that let her know he was merely joking.

She sighed happily. The whole family had welcomed her so openly. And they were all in on the secret that she was actually King Mandrake's daughter.

"The only person in the Western world who doesn't know at this point is King Mandrake himself," Jay said when the topic was broached. "Somebody is going to have to tell him at some point."

"Not now," Marco said. "Let him fume and threaten for the time being."

Shannon looked at him, wide-eyed. "This seems a new attitude for you," she said.

He shrugged. "I still feel beholden to the man, and I'll do all I can to make it up to him. But now that I've managed to step back, I'm pretty angry at the way he tried to palm his badly behaved daughter off on me. He obviously thought he could transfer all responsibility to someone else and wash his hands of her. And I don't think that's any way for a father to treat a daughter, no matter what she's done." He glanced over at where his own little Kiki was playing very nicely with a long-haired cat and his expression softened lovingly.

Shannon had smiled and nodded in total agreement. She knew she would have to face her father someday, but there was too much that was new going on in her life right now to give her much time to think about it.

"By the way," he'd told her. "Did you hear about Greta and Freddy?"

"No. You've heard something about them?"

He nodded. ''Mandrake wasn't pleased with the way they'd handled the problem with Iliana. He had them banished to a little town on the border. I hear they're running a bed and breakfast.''

Shannon had laughed along with the others, but she had a twinge of regret. After all, she'd had a part in the debacle, hadn't she?

But that had been three days ago. Now they were in the carriages, on the way to Red Rose Castle where the coronation would take place. After that ceremony, they would all ride back down to the crystal cathedral where the weddings would follow. And then the parties would begin.

Her heart was in her throat. She knew she was taking a series of huge steps with all the risks attached. She was marrying Marco—though that wasn't such a risk. It seemed like the most natural step she'd ever taken. She was becoming a mother to two little children, and that was natural as well. Could she become an instant mother? Yes! She knew she could. But could she step up and become a worthy queen? That one made her shiver a bit in her boots. Jay kept saying how brave she was and she was determined not to let her old friend down. She thought she could do it. Marco was sure she could do it. But only time would tell.

Her carriage was first in the procession, and each of the other brides, as well as Karina, was in a carriage behind hers, while the men rode ahead on horseback. Dressed in full medieval regalia, their formation was meant to echo the royal warrior groups who went out to fight the enemy in centuries past, with Marco riding at the head, his brothers fanned out behind him,

and then various relatives and advisors, each holding
a ceremonial place in the scheme of things. When
she'd first caught a glimpse of Marco in his dark blue
uniform her heart had skipped a beat. Had any man
ever been more handsome? Impossible!

Huge colorful banners celebrating the monarchy
flew in the wind along the way and people lined the
street, calling out and waving, even applauding as she
rode past.

"Do I have to wave like Queen Elizabeth?" she'd
asked Tianna that morning.

Tianna and Karina were working hard to make a
proper royal out of her, teaching her things Greta and
Freddy never even thought of.

"Wave however you want," Tianna had told her.
"Just be comfortable."

Mainly, she was smiling and nodding at the crowd,
even blowing kisses on occasion. Actually, she
couldn't stop smiling if she wanted to. It seemed to
be permanently affixed to her face by now.

She turned and looked back at Princess Tianna in
the carriage behind hers. Tianna gave her a smile and
a wink, as if to say, "Just have fun with this. It's all
part of the game."

This was wonderful. Not only was she gaining a
husband and two lovely children, but a sisterhood of
close friends like she'd never had before. She already
had special ties to each one of them. She felt a special
closeness with Sara because she seemed to have many
of the same down-to-earth qualities Shannon felt she
had herself. Plus, they both had been raised as com-
moners and were now attempting to fit into royal life.
Karina's interest in history and archiving jibed beau-

tifully with her passion for art history, and Tianna was a professional photographer who planned to document the transition the country was going through in line with her own work.

And then there were the men. Marco was her hero, her prince, soon to be her king and beloved husband. His brother Garth was such a rugged warrior, the sort of man you hoped to have at your side in any battle. Damian was a loveable playboy with a great sense of humor. And Jack Santini, Karina's husband, was even more good-looking than the Roseanova men, with his dark Italian looks and his keen intelligence. She loved them all, and that even included the duke and duchess of Gavini who were favorites of hers now.

The castle towered above her as her carriage came to a stop. A footman opened her carriage door and helped her to the red velvet carpet that let into the coronation hall. The men had already dismounted and were waiting in a sort of receiving line to escort each woman in. As she joined Marco, she smiled up into his face and he smiled down at her, but she could see something new in his gaze, something serious and filled with awe at what he was about to do. She wanted to say something warm and encouraging, but her heart was in her throat and she merely took his arm and let him begin to lead her in the slow, stately walk down the velvet carpet, into the great hall, past the many honored guests.

She took her seat in the front row and he bowed low, then turned and made his way to the center of the dais, directly facing two huge golden thrones. Shannon felt faint as she realized she would be sitting in one of those magnificent chairs very soon.

As soon as everyone was seated, the ceremony began and Shannon was swept up in the majesty of it all. There were prayers and proclamations, solemn anthems and a poetry reading, and then Marco was given an ermine cape with red velvet lining. Candles were lit, music was played, promises were made, and finally, Marco knelt at the steps to the platform where the thrones sat and the oldest member of the cabinet that had been in place twenty years before set a heavy, bejeweled crown on his head and placed a thick golden staff in his hand. Rising, he turned to look at his subjects and a sudden cheer rose from the crowd. The cheer caught on, swelling down into the street. Marco looked startled at first, then he smiled and raised his arms to the crowd. Shannon smiled, her heart full of love and pride in him, her eyes shimmering with tears. She was so glad she was here to watch him in this moment of his glory.

And soon she would be sharing it with him. They rose from their seats and returned to the carriages. Now the trip would be back down into the town where the wedding ceremonies would take place in the crystal cathedral. Time was going very quickly now. In less than an hour, she would be married to the king. She could hardly catch her breath.

"Here we are," said Jay, who was riding in the carriage with her as they arrived at the cathedral. "Get ready, my dear. It's your big moment."

Shannon turned, and going totally against protocol, threw her arms around the woman.

"Jay, if it weren't for you, none of this would be happening. I love you so much, and appreciate you even more. I'm so grateful."

Jay smiled at her with tears in her eyes. "I know my darling Lorraine is smiling down from heaven right now," she said in a broken voice. "I'm sure she is saying, 'Yes, Mother, this is the perfect choice. I love her, too.'

Shannon sobbed against her friend's shoulder, and Jay patted her and whispered, "Come on now, be a queen!"

Immediately she straightened and blinked her tears away. There was Marco, waiting to escort her into the cathedral as Nabotavian custom dictated. He looked so splendid now, so full of dignity and nobility. Would she ever be a proper match for him? If not, it wouldn't be for lack of trying. Rising regally, she held her head high and smiled at him.

"And may we all live happily ever after," Shannon said as she took Marco's arm and turned to look back at the others.

"Amen," he answered as their eyes met and the deep love they shared trembled between them. "Amen."

* * * * *

SILHOUETTE *Romance*®

introduces regal tales of love and honor in the exciting new miniseries

CATCHING THE CROWN

by Raye Morgan

When the Royal Family of Nabotavia is called to return to its native land after years of exile, the princes and princesses must do their duty. But will they meet their perfect match before it's too late?

Find out in:

JACK AND THE PRINCESS (#1655)
On sale April 2003

BETROTHED TO THE PRINCE (#1667)
On sale June 2003
and

COUNTERFEIT PRINCESS (#1672)
On sale July 2003

And don't miss the exciting story of Prince Damian of Nabotavia in
ROYAL NIGHTS

Coming in May 2003, a special Single Title found wherever Silhouette books are sold.

**Available at your favorite retail outlet.
Only from Silhouette Books!**

Where love comes alive™

If you enjoyed what you just read,
then we've got an offer you can't resist!

Take 2 bestselling
love stories FREE!
Plus get a FREE surprise gift!

Clip this page and mail it to Silhouette Reader Service™

IN U.S.A.
3010 Walden Ave.
P.O. Box 1867
Buffalo, N.Y. 14240-1867

IN CANADA
P.O. Box 609
Fort Erie, Ontario
L2A 5X3

YES! Please send me 2 free Silhouette Romance® novels and my free surprise gift. After receiving them, if I don't wish to receive anymore, I can return the shipping statement marked cancel. If I don't cancel, I will receive 6 brand-new novels every month, before they're available in stores! In the U.S.A., bill me at the bargain price of $3.34 plus 25¢ shipping and handling per book and applicable sales tax, if any*. In Canada, bill me at the bargain price of $3.80 plus 25¢ shipping and handling per book and applicable taxes**. That's the complete price and a savings of at least 10% off the cover prices—what a great deal! I understand that accepting the 2 free books and gift places me under no obligation ever to buy any books. I can always return a shipment and cancel at any time. Even if I never buy another book from Silhouette, the 2 free books and gift are mine to keep forever.

215 SDN DNUM
315 SDN DNUN

Name	(PLEASE PRINT)	
Address	Apt.#	
City	State/Prov.	Zip/Postal Code

* Terms and prices subject to change without notice. Sales tax applicable in N.Y.
** Canadian residents will be charged applicable provincial taxes and GST.
All orders subject to approval. Offer limited to one per household and not valid to current Silhouette Romance® subscribers.
® are registered trademarks of Harlequin Books S.A., used under license.

SROM02 ©1998 Harlequin Enterprises Limited

We're proud to present two emotional novels of
strong Western passions, intense, irresistible heroes
and the women who are about to
tear down their walls of protection!

Don't miss

SUMMER
Gold

containing

Sweet Wind, Wild Wind
by *New York Times* bestselling author
Elizabeth Lowell

&

A Wolf River Summer
an original novel by
Barbara McCauley

Available this June wherever Silhouette books are sold.

Silhouette®
Where love comes alive™

SILHOUETTE *Romance*®

COMING NEXT MONTH

#1678 BEAUTY & THE BEASTLY RANCHER—
Judy Christenberry
From the Circle K
Anna Pointer agreed to a marriage of convenience for the sake of her kids. After all, Joe Crawford was kind, generous—her children loved him—and he was handsome, too! But Joe thought he could only offer his money and his name. Could Anna convince her husband that he was her Prince Charming?

#1679 DISTRACTING DAD—Terry Essig
Nothing encourages romance like…*a flood?* When Nate Parker's dad accidentally flooded Allie MacLord's apartment, Nate let his beautiful neighbor bunk with him—but he had no intention of falling in love. But then neighborly affection included Allie's sweet kisses.…

#1680 JARED'S TEXAS HOMECOMING—
Patricia Thayer
The Texas Brotherhood
Jared Trager went to Texas to find his deceased brother's son—and became a stepfather to the boy! Dana Shayne thought Jared was a guardian angel sent to save her farm and her heart. But could she forgive his deceit when she learned his true intentions?

#1681 DID YOU SAY…*WIFE?*—Judith McWilliams
Secretary Joselyn Stemic was secretly in love with Lucas Tarrington—her sexy boss! So when an accident left Lucas with amnesia, she pretended to be his wife. At first it was just so the hospital would let her care for him—but what would happen when she took her "husband" home?

#1682 MARRIED IN A MONTH—Linda Goodnight
Love-shy rancher Colt Garret didn't know a thing about babies and never wanted a wife. Then he received custody of a two-month-old and desperately turned to Kati Winslow for help. Kati agreed to be the nanny for baby Evan…if Colt agreed to marry her in a month!

#1683 DAD TODAY, GROOM TOMORROW—Holly Jacobs
Perry Square
Louisa Clancy had left home eight years ago with a big check and an even bigger secret. She'd thought she put the past behind her—then Joe Delacamp came into her store and spotted *their* son. Was this long-lost love about to threaten all Louisa's dreams? Or would it fulfill her deepest longings…?

SRCNM0703